CONSCIENCE PLACE

Also by Joyce Thompson

MERRY-GO-ROUND

HOTHOUSE

35¢ THRILLS

THE BLUE CHAIR

CONSCIENCE PLACE

A NOVEL BY

Joyce Thompson

Doubleday & Company, Inc.
Garden City, New York

1984

All characters in this book are fictitious,
and any resemblance to persons living or dead
is entirely coincidental.

Library of Congress Cataloging in Publication Data
Thompson, Joyce.
Conscience Place.
I. Title.
PS3570.H6414C6   1984   813'.54
ISBN: 0-385-18864-1
Library of Congress Catalog Card Number 82–46073

First Edition

For the kids

I too felt the curious abrupt questionings stir within me,
In the day among crowds of people sometimes they
        came upon me,
In my walks home late at night or as I lay in bed they
        came upon me,
I too had been struck from the float forever held in
        solution,
I too had received identity by my body,
That I was I knew was of my body, and what I should be
        I knew I should be of my body.

Walt Whitman
from *Crossing Brooklyn Ferry*

CONSCIENCE PLACE

1

HERE THE MASCULINE IS UNIVERSAL. The pronoun *he* and its possessive *him* connote not sexual identity but simple sentient being. *I breathe, I exist, I am he.* In a place of infinite difference, language insists on sameness. If the brain lacks the tools of dialectic, it is reasoned, then only synthesis is possible. In a place of infinite deviation, language imposes normality. What the mind cannot frame in words, it does not know. The idea of deviation becomes an unthinkable thought.

The People. Most of their bodies carry sexual apparatus of some sort, have clitoris and cleft or penis and testicles, or both, but Eros is not one of the recognized or recognizable gods of the Place, so that when hormones sing and blood races, as they sometimes will, when tensile tissues prickle and rise up, as sometimes they must, the result is treated in custom and parlance as the Excitement, an individual state of spiritual exaltation whose physical symptoms are curious and incidental. There is no word for *sex* in the lexicon of the Place, nor for *passion, exploitation,* or *desire.* The Fathers needed to prevent conception and this seemed to them the most compassionate of ways for doing so. Successful union is the agreement of like minds.

The Excitement is one of the mysteries, one of those things which are accepted without challenge or any hope of explanation. The idea was considered, and rejected, of construing the Excitement as religious experience. Though the institution of religion traditionally acts as an effective stimulus to sublimation and as a powerful though subtle instrument of social control, it has also in the course of history proved itself to be

politically dangerous, capable of inspiring the unwaver-
ing conviction of which zealots are made, and for this
reason, the Fathers omitted it from the design as they
wove the social and ideologic fabric of the Place. Nature for the People is a first principle in place of a deity;
it is a force both inhuman and indisputable, and the
mysteries are its given laws.

The Fathers studied history long and hard in order to
extract its lessons and put them to use in the creation of
the Place. The greatest lesson they learned from history
was of the subversive nature of history. The language of
the Place has no tense perfect enough to extend the
past beyond reach of living memory. The People do not
read, nor can they write.

2

IN THE VIEWFINDER of the video camera, everything exists on the long gray spectrum between white and black. Light is the chisel that sculpts image from nothingness, and the shadows are as real as the light. Bartholomew doesn't mind, in fact, now that he's so well used to it, likes this second, monochrome perception, this universe of shape and density. By its austerity, he judges composition and exposure, far more clearly and critically than he might, subjected to the seductions of color. As soon as the technical estimations are made, judgments he now arrives at quickly and by intuition, just seconds later, his imagination colors the picture. The pool becomes blue/green again, a translucent fluid gemstone, rectangular and set in white tile, the bodies of the People warm to living brown or beige or yellow as they swim.

With his left hand, just as the woodwinds join the strings in the surrounding symphony, he pulls the lever and slowly, gently zooms in on Leda as he spirals through the water. The overheads are spots, their light is not diffuse but dapples Leda's long brownness silver as he passes in and out of their reach. Having only an upper right limb and a lower left, Leda swims like a spirochete, travels in water as a spinning bullet pierces air, torpedo-like. Bartholomew tracks him, his lens extended. When in mid-revolution Leda surfaces briefly for air, his face fills the screen, eyes closed and mouth gaping, with an expression so peculiarly ecstatic it makes Bartholomew think of the Excitement, of how it feels sometimes. Then he zooms out again, so his shot takes in the whole pool, and the bodies of the swimmers exist as pattern in their blue/green space. The limbless float, serenely immobile, while the swimmers dart among them, executing a complex water dance that relates their still forms with lines of motion. The movement swells to finale, and then the dance is done. While the watchers clap and cheer, Bartholomew records their reactions, a long wide shot and several close-ups, the happiness and wonder in their eyes.

Whether he'll edit the tape or run it as is, Bartholomew has not decided yet. The event is covered adequately, even well—of that he's sure—but lately, a new impulse dogs him, a wish to juxtapose seemingly unrelated images, to compare visually things that are, by word, incomparable. The swimmers remind him of birds. Bartholomew watches birds, he contemplates them. Bartholomew photographs birds and dreams of flying.

It is not easy to make pictures of birds in flight. There are trade-offs involved: the freedom and quickness of the body versus the stability of a tripod. There is the problem of shooting into the sun. And birds are shy; they seem to fear the camera. Its purpose is benign, the mechanism voiceless, but they flee it, they fly away when they see his lens is trained on them. To photograph birds requires patience and discretion. Sometimes for hours, Bartholomew sits hidden and motionless until his prey, his prey of images, comes into view.

A small poolside derrick lifts Leda from the water and deposits him in the waiting chair. Deftly, one-handed, he towels his long brown body dry, spreads the towel over his one leg and wheels himself up to Bartholomew, already beginning to pack up his equipment. As most of the People, Leda is fascinated by television and loves to see his picture on the screen. No matter how many times Bartholomew explains that it is not mysterious, is simply a matter of smart machines intelligently used, most of the People count television among the mysteries. They count Bartholomew, who makes television, a sort of priest or wizard, one who traffics on a daily basis with the unknown.

Leda preens, his head cocked sideways as he looks at Bartholomew. "Did you like the dance?" Leda asks. "Did you take my picture?"

"Yes," Bartholomew says. "Yes." With his left hand, flesh and bone, he wraps the mike cord around the shiny metal of his mechanical right hand. Yesses are not enough; Leda wheedles. "I'm available for an interview."

The birds in Bartholomew's mind fly away. Leda is lobbying for documentary. Show the event as it took place. I will tell you how I feel about making the dance, and you will tell the People. Bartholomew would like to be something more, something different from a good reporter, which he is, the what he cannot say, but he will be reporter, too. He plugs the mike back into the recorder. "Sound only," he tells Leda. "The camera's put away. I can run your voice over the dance."

Leda pouts, then shrugs, one-shouldered. Before he dresses, he'll put his prostheses on; the metal sockets to receive them lie waiting, embedded in his flesh. Bartholomew extends the microphone and nods.

"First comes the music." Leda's voice is more lyrical, more formal than in ordinary conversation. "I close my eyes and listen to the music. I play the music when I swim. I begin to hear the movements of the dance inside the music. The music tells me how the dance should be." Leda looks at Bartholomew for permission to continue and getting it, goes on. "I hear the quiet places in the music, I hear little silences, and this gives me the idea to put the limbless ones in the dance."

Bartholomew is interested in spite of himself. "How do they fit together?" he asks. "How do you know?"

"I feel it," Leda says. "Sometimes when I swim, my brain makes up music. It can happen both ways."

"It's different from the dance of the chairs," Bartholomew says, intending to spur Leda on. Leda moves hungrily toward the mesh head of the microphone.

"The chairs go right or left, forward or back. The chairs are limited. In water, we have freedom."

Bartholomew thinks again of birds. Sometime, not now, he would like to ask Leda if he thinks his dance is like the flight of birds. He switches off the recorder and smiles.

"That's all?" Leda says.

"That's all," Bartholomew says. "I have other things to do." It takes a certain amount of time, he knows, to strike his equipment and that long, at least, to set it up again. His body, confined to the chair, requires so much time. To Bartholomew, it is neither easier nor harder than it should be, but only how it is. He hangs the recorder and battery pack on a special bracket on the back of his chair, cradles the camera in his lap and rolls away, down the ramp and out of the poolhouse.

The outside path is rougher than the poolhouse ramps; he can feel the resistance it offers to his wheels. It is a fine day of the third season. The autumn weather is a filter, a subtle color shift away from the vibrancy of summer with its white-hot light. The shadows are crisper now and more delicate, the air cool enough to sting Bartholomew's cheeks. He rolls toward the compound and Brother Alice, past the dwelling houses and the kitchens, beyond the gymnasium and playing fields and gardens. At this time of day, the People work. The paths are empty.

Passing into the garden, he hears the clatter that

means birds, seeks out the sound and finds its source aloft, two ducks sailing black against the blue/white sky. As if they sense an audience, the ducks linger to perform, drawing a thin silent oval against the high clouds then braking, their bodies arched against the wind, wings forward, flapping. The ducks descend and then, in unison, they stop the fall, stretch forward like swimmers and stroke toward the sun. There is no time to ready the camera, no way to catch and keep the moment. He shoots it anyway; with his camera eye, he frames and tracks them, recklessly follows their flight across the sun. Radiant circles burn into his vision and persist when he lowers his eyes. Slowly they cool to black and he can see again. The ducks are gone. Bartholomew sits a moment longer, mourning the lost image, and then rolls on.

It is seasons past now when Bartholomew asked Brother Alice to name the birds for him and Brother Alice said, "Their name is birds."

Bartholomew said, "The birds are different. Some are big and some are small. Some are black, some are red or blue. Some birds have many colors."

Brother Alice looked at Bartholomew through eyes like staggered lenses. "The People are all different, but we are all the People," Brother Alice said.

"We have names," Bartholomew persisted. "I'm Bartholomew. Leda is Leda. Who chooses our names?"

"Language is the gift of the Fathers," Brother Alice told him. Sometime later, he told Bartholomew that the Fathers had decided to name the birds. "If you bring me the pictures you take of birds, I'll ask the Fathers for their names." In this way Bartholomew learned crow and duck, robin, sparrow and goldfinch. The small bird with fast thistle wings is called a hummingbird, the big hoarse blue one is a jay.

He goes to Brother Alice now. Once each day he goes to Brother Alice and Brother Alice tells him if there is anything at the Place he should make television of. If there is nothing, Bartholomew can shoot whatever pleases him. Most often, there is some assignment—an interview, a dance or game to be recorded, a message from Brother Alice that must be taped. Twice a day, before breakfast and after dinner, Bartholomew's tapes are shown on television; the rest of the time, the sets are part of the intricate communication web that connects the People. Bartholomew can dial Leda and see and hear him; Leda can dial Brother Alice; through television all of the People can meet together at once. The blind can hear it, the deaf and speechless watch. Even the limbless ones can use television easily.

Brother Alice is smaller in the shoulders and chest than Bartholomew, though unlike Bartholomew, he has legs and can walk by himself. His skin is silver and scaled, like the bright skin of a fish. Round and green, big as three ordinary human eyes, Brother Alice's right eye is positioned on his face several centimeters higher than his left one. This green eye never moves or blinks. Bartholomew imagines it is the fixed lens of a camera; to change the shot, the whole head has to move. Bartholomew imagines, too, that this eye sees more deeply than other eyes; he has always assumed that Brother Alice sees meaning as well as manifest event, but has always been too shy to ask if this is true.

Brother Alice has one solid and useful arm, on his left, and one smaller limb, handless and without joints, useful only for crude tasks or in the swimming tank. Today, Brother Alice's smock is bright orange. Today, reflections of the orange smock tinge his silver scales with orange. He greets Bartholomew wordlessly, with an inclination of the head, as if he were welcome but not important. Brother Alice wears earphones and listens intently to their message. Bartholomew wonders if it is the Fathers who speak to him.

At first, when he removes the headset, he simply looks at Bartholomew and smiles. The scrutiny is disconcerting; Bartholomew feels as if he were naked, inside and out, under that gaze. Many of the People fear Brother Alice, though none dislikes him. He is different from the others and alone among them in having power. The Fathers speak to him and, through him, to the People. His word is the reality of the Place. And Brother Alice is beautiful. Other of the People have scales, but none so silver; there are many shapes and kinds of eyes, but none so penetrating or so green as his.

When he speaks, Brother Alice's voice is lightly melodious. "How is the water dance?" he asks.

"It moved me," Bartholomew says. "I like it."

"I was sorry to miss it. I'm glad you have pictures. Will you show them tonight?"

"I don't know," Bartholomew says. Brother Alice's higher eye demands more answer. "I might edit," he goes on. "I might add other pictures."

"What pictures?"

"Of birds," Bartholomew says.

"Do you ever think of anything besides birds, Bartholomew?"

The moving blue eye laughs, but the fixed green eye continues stern. Bartholomew feels a warmth rise in his face, as if the sun were shining under his skin. "I think about light," he says, "and trees. Sometimes I think about insects."

"And I suppose soon you'll be wanting names for those things too."

The statement is half question, half joke. Bartholomew *would* like names for the trees and insects, but is

ashamed to want so much. Already he has his own
names for light, names made up from color words and
feeling words. He doesn't say so, simply nods.

"The Fathers have more important things to do than
name the insects for you, Bartholomew. There are
more insects than People. Did you know that?"

Bartholomew has guessed this might be true, but he
says no.

"If there's ever time, I might ask the Fathers about
the trees. Would you like that?"

Bartholomew says yes. He says thank you. Brother
Alice continues to regard him, his two eyes differently
unsettling. Paintings and photographs made by the
People hang on the white walls of Brother Alice's room,
and Bartholomew looks at these—at the image of a leaf,
valiantly yellow in the gray light of late autumn, afloat
in a still, dull puddle, and at Clotho's portrait of Brother
Alice, of the colors of Brother Alice. The green eye is
fiercely green, his lips red as a wound, his smock a clear
medium blue. The light makes rainbows on his silver
skin. The portrait is peaceful and unchanging, and Bartholomew often finds it easier to look at the picture
than at its living subject. His mind herds all the questions he would like to and will not ask.

When Brother Alice speaks again, it is to give Bartholomew assignments. "Tonight," he says, "we expect
to receive a new batch of nestlings. They will be
named. Tomorrow Ringer comes of age. These events
must be recorded." Though high, his voice is strong.
The strength of the person speaks in his voice. Bartholomew would not dream of disrespecting it. He nods:
understands: will do his duty. To make television is his
work.

Brother Alice dismisses him now with a curt nod of
his silver head. Leaving, Bartholomew feels vaguely

that he has missed a chance by not pushing his questions into the silence that Brother Alice allowed to pass between them. It was the longest pause of a long relationship, and as it was happening, Bartholomew feared it. Now that it's past, he wonders what revelations he has lost. His flesh hand trembles on the levers of his chair. Curiosity does not hold him; he rolls away from appraisal and invitation, to the cool space of his studio.

3

LIFE DOES NOT BEGIN AT THE PLACE, it arrives there. Without births, the number of the People grows. At no predictable interval, nestlings are brought by the Fathers to fill the nursery. As few as three, as many as a dozen or more, nestlings always arrive in batches, each one small and helpless, each one unique. The nestlings cry, and the People understand that there is anguish at life's beginning. This is thought to be the result of pain at separation from the Fathers.

The pain passes and life is shown to be good. At its end, when one is summoned back, the People grieve for him, but the one who returns to the Fathers does not cry.

The nurture and education of the nestlings is given in part to the small ones, for to nurture and educate others is to grow oneself. No rigid syllabus guides learning here, where education has the twin goals of self-discovery and self-sufficiency; to study is to seek one's talents and an understanding of how to use them. Because each of the People is bodily different, his education is different from all others. Nothing is mass-produced, nor is it possible to assume that the tools and techniques a limbless one uses to paint, or to eat, or to move from place to place are the best and most efficient tools and techniques for all. Those who exhibit aptitude for mechanical invention are trained from smallness to design the apparatus that helps others to use their talents and to fulfill their basic needs.

To come of age at the Place is to receive the tools and prostheses of adult life. The bodies of the small ones are too frail to bear the weight of artificial limbs, which are, in any case, too soon outgrown. When the growth curve has peaked and begins to flatten, when the body stabilizes at maturity, then one is taken to the doctors and fitted for those parts and pieces which will provide a maximum of mobility, of utility and independence for the rest of his life.

The doctors are, to the People, beings nearly as mythical as the Fathers. No one has ever seen them or heard them speak. After a time of fasting and meditation, the new initiate is given a drug which erases consciousness, and memory with it. His sleep is dreamless. At its end, the sleeper wakes to a new body, wrought of flesh and ingenuity. For a few days he stays on at the doctor's house, while nurses, who are of the People, help him to master the use of his new parts and tell him all the doctors have said that he must know. His return to the People is marked by celebration. That the Excitement is first experienced at or around the time one receives his prostheses is thought to be a spiritual confirmation of physical maturity, and is reckoned among the mysteries.

4

LUCAS WITH HIS FINE VOICE gives them names. He does not make up the names, which come from the Fathers; they are whispered to him, and he is the first to speak the names out loud among the People. His voice connects word to body. It is his speaking of the names which makes them belong to the nestlings.

Even among the People, Lucas seems an exceptional being, a daring experiment of the Fathers, whose very success seems proof of special grace. His is a large head, with high-placed eyes, slashed by a huge mouth his whole jaw wide, the great mouth through which his great voice speaks. Below his big skull and short broad neck, Lucas has no skeleton or skin. His organs, perfect and whole, are permanently suspended in a large cylinder of transparent plastic, bathed in life-sustaining fluid of a clear teal blue and lit, so all the People can see and appreciate internal mysteries—the swelling and deflation of his lungs; the energetic, rhythmical contraction of his muscle-heart; the long opalescent coil of his intestines.

Lucas takes food and air by mouth. A wing-shaped sac of clear plastic, carefully sealed, protects his trachea and lungs from drowning in the surrounding fluid, and a small pump that works with a regular, audible sigh helps his lungs rise and fall. To remove wastes from the system, the nurses plug tubes into the sockets which stud his cylinder and hook Lucas up to a suction machine several times a day. The rest of the time, he is mobile, since his cylinder has wheels, though dependent on the strength and willingness of others to move him from place to place.

The visiting room of the nursery is gently lit to soothe the nestlings and Bartholomew opens his lens to use what light there is. The People form a circle, those who can, standing, the others in their chairs or on their carts, with Lucas shining grandly at their center. Loud and solemnly, he speaks a name, and as he does, one of the nurses carries the nestling who will wear that name around the circle, pausing long enough for each of the People to welcome the new one in his own fashion— with a smile, a touch, a snatch of singing or a simple, silent inclination of the head. For steadiness, Bartholomew uses the tripod. He follows each of the nestlings— this time there are four—around the circle in his turn.

Neither his presence nor the camera's distracts the People; they ignore Bartholomew, while the power of his lens makes him party to each intimate transaction. When the tape is shown later, others not present now will share in the event. Because the People are many and the visiting room is small, only a representative few, chosen by lot, can take part in any naming. Only Bartholomew because of his camera and Lucas with his voice are privileged to be present at every ceremony.

The names of those who have returned to the Fathers are sometimes sent back for the nestlings. When Lucas calls out "Desdemona," small gasps and sighs arise, and the nestling Desdemona is greeted tenderly. Desdemona, who was and is gone, was quick to laugh and talented in sport. He is remembered and missed, and Bartholomew thinks the Fathers are wise to give the People back his name. He zooms in on the small one, until his dusky, puckered face fills all the frame, and this close-up is a caress, Bartholomew's own gesture of welcome.

When the naming is done, Desdemona, Leroy, Ethel, and Hanford have joined the People. While there is time, Bartholomew spends some tape on Lucas, on the clear bubbles rising in his blue fluid, the wash of his gleaming viscera, lit and glowing in the dimness. These images are extraneous to the event, but Lucas is so oddly beautiful, so exquisitely strange that Bartholomew cannot resist shooting. The nestlings are carried back to the nursery, the lights come up, the People break their circle and reform in smaller clusters to talk awhile before dispersing. Bartholomew would like to join them, to discuss the new arrivals and wonder, with the rest, how they will grow and who they will become, but turns instead to the inevitable chore of packing his machines.

Lucas calls out to him. Bartholomew turns to find him alone at the center of the broken circle and goes to him. Close to Lucas, he can hear the murmur of his lung pump. The commanding voice sounds plaintive. "The People forget about me when my job is done," he says.

Bartholomew understands what it is to feel set apart. Lightly, he taps the plastic cylinder, even though he knows Lucas can't feel his touch. "They respect you," he says. "It was a good ceremony."

"Push me over there," Lucas says. "Take me to Clotho and the others."

Bartholomew complies, as he is honor-bound to do. No request for assistance must be denied, nor does the person asking ever say please or give thanks. The People exist for one another. It is Lucas's right to ask for help. Chairs move and bodies shift to make room when he joins the cluster. Clotho, belly-flat on his cart, lifts his head to greet Lucas. "Soon I think I will be a good enough artist to paint even your picture, giver of names," Clotho says. His estrangement cured, Lucas laughs, a childlike gurgle.

Bartholomew returns to his equipment and pursues

his solitary work. By the time the recorder is hung securely on its bracket, the People are gone. Only one nurse remains, waiting to shut off the lights. "The new ones are beautiful," Bartholomew tells him. "Take care of them."

"As we cared for you," the nurse says. "Good night, Bartholomew."

Before he's reached the bottom of the ramp, the nursery goes dark behind him, the long rectangles of light its windows cast on the path disappear, as if a great eye has blinked and will not open. For a moment, Bartholomew is blind in the darkness, until the lens opens and the director that is his brain informs the optic nerves they will be shooting night for night. Slowly the shapes of trees appear, of houses, and he can see the path as it stretches out before him.

In the studio, Bartholomew rewinds the tape and files it. If he is not orderly by nature, he has become so by habit. The medium demands it. The machines he works with are sensitive and require meticulous care, the tapes are fragile and easy to damage. Besides, chaos wastes effort, and even when done efficiently, the work is repetitious. Bartholomew lives and lives again (again, again) every moment of real time that he records. Only by passionate fidelity to tedious routine can he be the single-person enterprise he is.

He should look at tonight's tape now, should make his rough cut, remove the self-indulgent close-ups of Lucas's insides, for a start, take out the underexposures—there are bound to be a few—and other technical mistakes. He *should* do that, but instead and somewhat guiltily, he puts up his tape of the water dance on one monitor and for the other selects a sequence from his library of birds. The cassettes click into place and the first frame of each tape appears as a still picture on its

monitor. Chance matches them: one high-flying goose
and a wide shot of the pool, just as Leda enters the
water. The jet of drops sprayed up on impact hangs a
shimmering V above the surface.

Bartholomew wheels himself to the shelf that is his
music library and scans the pictographs that label the
tapes. Each is identified with a small hand-drawn doo-
dle of some image suggested by the music on it. He has
no names for the pieces of music and doesn't know who
made them, but only how the music sounds and makes
him feel. What music has both air and water in it?
Which best connects the two? The choice is hard and
his selection tentative—a piece that combines the glide
of violins, the flights of piccolo and trills of flutes with
the deeper, more resonant voices of the bigger horns
and lower strings, with a booming kettledrum percussion that reminds him of sounds heard underwater, at
the bottom of the pool. He knows the instruments not
by their names but by their voices. This music was
given by the Fathers.

He puts his selection on the tape deck and begins it,
turning the volume loud enough to make the music fill
his brain and silence word-thoughts. The pictures, too,
he sets in motion: the goose flies; Leda swims. Bartholomew watches both together, and his senses are almost
dangerously filled. The display confirms his intuition—
even seen so crudely, without editing, there *is* corre-
spondence, a flirtation between the images. When ser-
endipity casts up pictures parallel in movement and
composition, Bartholomew stops both tapes, rewinds
and begins a slow dissolve. Leda dives and swims underwater, his body distorted by water-bent light. Just as
he surfaces, a duck springs up from the blue surface of
the lake, takes flight. Bartholomew runs it again and
again, manipulating the lever with utmost delicacy un-

til he has it right, until the two motions are perfectly continuous and describe one arc.

It is too good to lose. He stops the tapes, feeds a blank into the third recorder, rewinds, repeats the dissolve, previews and takes it. A keep. Something new exists in the world now—a swimmer has become a bird—and Bartholomew feels both humble and arrogant, to be the agent of the change. The music plays on and sounds impatient. He starts the videotapes and lets them race after it. Soon the dance of images seduces him and he watches, too transfixed now to exercise his power to meddle and transpose.

He simply watches. His nerves sing as he watches. He dives and flies. An excitement fills him, and his feeling of overload, of too much input, slowly transforms itself into a lack, a sense of longing. Slowly he understands it is the onset of the Excitement, a gift not of the Fathers but of nature itself, of his own senses and their capacity for joy. It is not the first time his work has brought him to the edges of the Excitement, and he is not bewildered or ashamed.

Bartholomew switches off the studio light and turns the music up as high as it will go, until he perceives it almost as a kind of pain. While the images fly by on their twin screens, he opens the front of his loose-fitting trousers, with his one warm fleshly hand finds the localized sites of the Excitement and touches each in turn: pert, firm clitoris and taut, hot penis. The firing of nerves is staggered slightly, the smaller part comes first, in a concentric ring of spasms that expands until it encompasses the second organ, and it too hits the top, gives way to the Excitement in a sharp, single burst of joy. Bartholomew adds his own cry to the voices of the music.

For some time he drifts wordlessly, sunk in the damp

delirium that follows the Excitement. The sound of his own breathing is louder than music in his ears. Slowly it quiets, slowly his skin prickles dry and he begins to enter the stone-cool, peaceful place that is as much a part of passion as its hot peaks, a deep green valley that is profoundly calm. Only then do his senses grow acute enough to tell him that someone else is present in the room. Brother Alice stands like a shadow beside the door, his scales absorbing light. The placid valley vanishes. Bartholomew feels heat radiant under the skin of his face, so hot and bright he wonders if it makes him glow. Discreetly as he can, he fumbles to close the fly of his trousers.

He must turn on the light, he must turn down the music. The music is so loud it hurts his ears. He turns the knob until the music shrinks, and the room seems to shrink, too. Its walls, stretched by sound, snap back in place and it seems easier to breathe. When he turns toward the light switch, Brother Alice stops him. He leaves his place beside the door and sits down facing the monitors where birds still fly and swimmers swim. Bartholomew rolls into place beside him, and together they watch the tapes play out. When they click off, Bartholomew turns on the light.

Brother Alice continues to stare at the blank screens. "It's hard," he says, "to see two things at once."

"Only at first," Bartholomew tells him. "You get used to it. Besides, when I'm done editing, the two tapes will be one."

"I look forward to seeing it."

Bartholomew looks at Brother Alice. "Is there something you want me to do?"

Brother Alice shakes his head. "I decided to go out for a walk, and when I came to the studio, I decided to see if you were here."

Brother Alice has never come without some purpose. He has never come at night. "I'm here," Bartholomew says.

"You love your work," Brother Alice says, and now his blue eye looks at Bartholomew. He feels no need to answer. Brother Alice says, "I envy you."

Bartholomew is surprised to learn that Brother Alice, by his own admission, is capable of feeling such a base emotion. "Don't you love yours?" he asks.

Brother Alice answers immediately, each of his eyes elusive, his scales the sad blue of his smock. "I love the idea of my work," he says, "but my work is hard. It isn't easy for me to see two things at once."

Bartholomew puzzles it out. "You mean the People and the Fathers?"

Brother Alice's red lips make a slow smile. "I suppose that's what I mean."

Brother Alice has always seemed to Bartholomew to know precisely what he means. That he too must guess makes the world seem less solid than Bartholomew imagined it to be. "But your work is very important," he insists.

"So is your work," Brother Alice says, but Bartholomew doesn't want to think about his own work. Aware that he presumes, he asks, "Are the Fathers difficult?"

"They can be difficult."

Bartholomew gives his imagination to the problem. "It must be hard to live in both the place of the Fathers and the place of the People."

"I live in the Place of the People."

"Then you must miss the Fathers." Bartholomew knows he speaks of things beyond his understanding. He speaks with no authority.

"I live with the People," Brother Alice says, "but I am not of the People." Bartholomew hears desolation in the sweet voice, and he understands for the first time that Brother Alice must be lonely. His words do not say so, not quite, the message is in his voice. Bartholomew does what the code of the People requires: made aware of need, he gives what help he can. Timidly, he moves closer to Brother Alice, close enough to reach his arm around the silver shoulders. He hopes he has not misunderstood.

Brother Alice hangs his head and allows himself to be hugged. Bartholomew's hand and arm, too discreet to collect and transmit sensory information about Brother Alice to his brain, go numb. They sit like stones. At last, Brother Alice moves his head to look at Bartholomew's hand where it rests on his shoulder. He raises his whole arm and lays his silver hand on Bartholomew's hand. There is a little roughness to his scales, a coolness to his skin. The touch is light, gone. Bartholomew understands that he can move his arm now.

"I'm sorry," Brother Alice says, and Bartholomew answers with words that are not his, but all the People's. "There is no shame in asking for help. We live to help each other."

Bartholomew speaks solemnly, but Brother Alice laughs. He laughs as if he believes the wisdom of the code does not apply to him, then rises and leaves the studio with no good-bye.

Alone, Bartholomew turns by habit to his machines. He presses buttons and, once again, pictures of the duck's rise and Leda's dive appear on the monitors, beautiful in their stillness. He can hear the music clearly again, and the notes of the high horns sound like wind.

5

A GIFT, at the Place, is an expression of the giver. By his mind and by his body it is made. Into it, he puts not only the best of what he is, but of what he can become. In making a gift, the giver is expected to stretch his talents to their greatest extent. To give is to make, to make is to grow. No gift is of value which is not an investment, an enlargement, of self.

A celebration is an occasion for giving. Some time before one comes of age, ten of the People are chosen by lot to make gifts for him. The paintings which result, the songs, dances, sculptures, inventions or discoveries are given to the celebrant in the name of all the People. Achievements of many selves in recognition of one, they belong to all the People, too. To receive a gift imparts responsibility: one must accept with pleasure and meet the gift with willingness to understand both its process and its intention. Each step of creation, from the first idea through the minutest detail of its execution, is part of what is given. The meaning of a gift must be sought and valued as highly as its form.

It is more important to be worthy of than grateful for a gift.

6

EARLY IN THE MORNING, long before the celebration is due to begin, Bartholomew visits each of the givers to ask them about their gifts. Louis the cook is hard at work in the kitchen, orchestrating among pots and pans, textures and smells, consistency, density, temperature and flavor a one-time-only edible accomplishment. In Ringer's honor, he has refined the flavoring of his egg sauce to new heights of piquancy. He will serve it with broccoli and call it Ringer's Sauce.

Ernestine has made up a play for Ringer, which five of the People perform together. In the play one of the People, who is named Geoffrey, dies. There is no real Geoffrey among the People—the name is made up— but the character is enough like Desdemona for the People to find the skeleton of truth inside the fiction. The play will make some of the People cry, those who were closest to Desdemona and miss him most, those who still have not resigned themselves to his loss. His gift, Ernestine says, is of catharsis, a release from the prison of grief.

Clotho has painted a picture. Bartholomew asks him what it is a picture of, and Clotho responds that it is a picture of what it feels like to be without limbs. Green, black, and bright clear yellow cover the canvas in swirls. Near the bottom of the picture is an angry splash of red. Lacking hands and feet, Clotho paints with brushes held between his teeth.

Adolph has perfected a new routine on the uneven parallel bars in Ringer's honor. Nearly all the time that Bartholomew talks with him, Adolph hangs by his knees from the lower bar, and Bartholomew, looking through the viewfinder at his upside-down face, feels himself grow a little dizzy. When he mentions it, Adolph laughs and begins to swing back and forth, his face leaving the frame, then growing larger and larger until his features are lost in a close-up too extreme.

Beatrice is a mime. Since one of the requirements of his medium is spontaneity, his gift does not yet exist when Bartholomew comes to see him. An instant will call it into being, though it is fed by hours of practice and years of observation. "My real gift is my readiness," he says. As Bartholomew interviews him, Beatrice paints his whole face starkly white.

Fabian the gardener cuts the finest of his flowers and arranges a bouquet for Ringer.

In the darkroom, Pavlova prints three portraits of Ringer—one as a nestling, one as a small one, one taken only a short time before—on the same paper. The current face is bigger and darker than the others; the face of the child is smaller, fainter, and of the baby, almost a ghost.

Darwin has made a song for four voices. His own is resonantly bass. Bartholomew records them as they practice their harmonies.

Lupe's gift is a larger than life-size sculpture of a fantastical prosthesis, a leg limb built of wire and meant to hang like a mobile, from the ceiling.

Ruth is a weaver, his flesh hand deft. To make his work easier, Boris the inventor has fashioned several attachments that fit directly into his prosthesis—a spinning wheel of small circumference, and a little loom. For Ringer, Ruth weaves a tapestry of subtle coloration and bold design.

And so the gifts are catalogued; when the tapes are shown, the People will be able to share the insights of the givers. Now Bartholomew returns to the dining hall to set up his equipment before the celebration begins. As he does so, one of Louis's assistants comes out of the kitchen and calls to him, "Come here. Louis wants to see you."

Bartholomew obeys. In the kitchen he finds Louis and his apprentices sampling the meal. Later, serving the others, they won't have time to eat. An extra place is set at the table. "Join us," Louis tells Bartholomew. "My sauce is too good to miss." Bartholomew eats with double pleasure, first at the food, which is superb, fresh and full of surprises, again at having cheerful company for his meal. The cooks talk cooking, laughing often at jokes whose humor depends on an understanding of the properties of foodstuffs, which he lacks, but he joins the laughter anyway in a simple spirit of goodwill. Ringer's Sauce is so subtle and intriguing that Bartholomew closes his eyes as he tastes it, giving all his attention to the small euphonies and confrontations between salt and hot and citron. When he licks his lips and looks up, he finds that Louis is watching and looks proud.

The great bell rings. In the kitchen, the tableau of cooks springs into motion. Bartholomew races into the hall, wheels fast on the smooth tile, and rescues his equipment just before the first wave arrives to engulf it. The platform is round and occupies the very center of the hall. It rotates slowly, so all the People in turn can see equally well what takes place on it. The small table where Ringer will eat alone among his friends is set and waiting. Bartholomew unpacks the portable tripod that Boris designed for him and bolts it to the arm of his chair. It was an excellent gift, called into being by an observed need; now Bartholomew has mobility and stability at once, and his work is better for it.

The dining tables are great notched circles set concentrically around the platform. Each has arcs where the places are matched with chairs, and arcs with none, where those in wheelchairs can approach the table. At one arc of each table, there is a small derrick and special chairs where the limbless can be strapped upright, and beside the special chairs, spaces for those who feed the limbless ones. Always these places fill quickly; no one is required to feed the limbless, but everyone is willing to help.

The crowd radiates out from the platform. Laughter and conversation rise in concentric rings of sound, and Bartholomew wishes, not for the first time, there were some way to capture its circularity, but his microphone is less sophisticated than his ears, and the tapes give back at best a pallid echo of what he hears at the center of the circle.

When all are assembled, the great bell tolls again. Silence falls in circles, until the very heart is quiet. Then Ringer comes to fill his empty place, the white cloak wrapped tight around him to hide the innovations until all can see at once. A murmur rises and follows him; he walks. For the first time in his life, he walks, and his gait is ragged, as it will be until his body and his brain have time to accommodate the change, to get used to the prosthesis and the process of walking, but still, the sight is thrilling. As always on such occasions, Bartholomew feels a vicarious tingle in his useless lower limbs, in the back of his mouth a small vapor that tastes like envy. He swallows it down, so his happiness for Ringer will be unspoiled.

Bartholomew follows the initiate's march to the platform in his viewfinder, raises the camera and zooms out just far enough so that Ringer's whole body is visible in the moment of drama. Ringer unfurls the cape and stands before the People in his new-made form. His prosthetic leg gleams coolly of steel. Its form, precise and elegant, makes it seem more perfect and ingenious than his nature-leg, its shape half obscured by the silky light brown hair that grows from it. Such hair, a luxuriant coat, covers all of Ringer's body except the small mobile mask of his face, creased now in a deep grin.

Bartholomew zooms in to examine Ringer's prosthetic hand as he displays its properties. Slowly, with almost excruciating care, the metal digits close around a drinking glass; the new hand must grip tightly enough to hold but not to break. When the necessary balance is achieved, Ringer raises the glass to the People and they applaud him. Bartholomew moves his chair slightly to pan the arcs of People cheering.

Brother Alice rises at his place in the first arc and signals Lucas, who calls out, "Let the feast begin!" A small army of servers carries huge bowls and platters of food to the People, while Louis himself serves Ringer, arranging the food on his plate as though it were a circular collage. Bartholomew focuses on Louis's hands as he spoons sauce onto the vegetables, on the delicate greens and yellows, the sauce spreading like a fluid blanket over the long stalks with their dark green curly heads, on the clear wine filling Ringer's glass. Louis speaks and they both laugh, though Bartholomew's microphone is too far away and too insensitive to catch the joke.

Ringer takes up a fork with his new hand, separates broccoli flowers from broccoli stalk and guides the morsel surely to his mouth. A virtuoso performance; once again the People cheer him.

Now the others begin to eat, too, and Bartholomew makes a slow pan of the diners, recording their reactions to the meal. A few, as he did, close their eyes better to experience the pleasures of the sauce.

While the eating goes on, Beatrice the mime appears,

white-faced, among the People. First he climbs on the platform, sits on an invisible chair across the table from Ringer and, wielding imaginary utensils, makes himself the mirror image of Ringer eating, exaggerates the movements of his jaw, wipes an imaginary fleck of sauce from imaginary fur. Self-conscious, Ringer grins, he ducks his head, he covers his face with his hands, but the mirror will not be evaded. Ringer sticks out his tongue at Beatrice, and Beatrice becomes Ringer sticking out his tongue at Beatrice. So quick is Beatrice, so kinesthetically prescient that there seems to be no lag between the movements of subject and mime. The People howl with delight.

For a long time, Bartholomew holds a simple two-shot, the camera as transfixed as his eye, before he remembers that he too practices an art. His job is not only to record but to discover. He moves in tight on Beatrice, so that the camera can explore beyond what changes to what remains the same. Beatrice has nostrils but no nose, hearing holes but no external earflaps. Beneath the stark, subtractive makeup, his face seems minimal, a face of infinite possibilities, none realized, yet even as the camera probes and questions, his face becomes Ringer's, his mouth and eyes laugh Ringer's laugh. Bartholomew makes the camera travel downward, to show how Beatrice maintains a sitting posture without a chair, how he becomes himself a chair, his prosthetic leg rigid, his real leg trembling with the effort of rigidity. Four huge screens suspended from the ceiling, one on each wall, project the images live as Bartholomew shoots them. The People share his explorations.

At last, Beatrice rises and bows to Ringer. Fabian brings his flowers and places them on Ringer's table. Clotho presents his painting and Pavlova his photograph. Lupe's sculpture descends from the ceiling above the platform, the play is played. One by one the gifts come and Bartholomew frames them in the viewfinder and gives them to the People. He gives them Ringer, too, enlarging his visible joy until his grin shines large on the four walls and surrounds them. Only the final gift remains to be given, and this one comes from Brother Alice. It is the gift of work.

Each of the People, coming of age, is given his vocation, and none resents the choice being made for him because it is, finally, *his* choice, work chosen to match his aptitudes and predilections, work that will serve the community and encourage the individual to grow. Thus Louis, who as a small one loved to eat, became a cook; Leda, who swam at every chance, was chosen to make water dances and to teach others to swim; Beatrice, who made fun of his playmates, now mirrors the idiosyncrasies of his fellows. Small Bartholomew was a chronic watcher. Now he shares his observations. All work has value, and all the People wonder what Ringer's will be in the moments before Brother Alice rises to make it known.

Side by side on the platform, Brother Alice is small and Ringer large, yet no one would confuse the wise one with the new initiate. Brother Alice shines silver-purple in his purple smock. Ringer stands awkwardly on his new leg and asks the ritual question: What is my work?

"Your work, Ringer, is to make television. Bartholomew will teach you. You will be his assistant, and then his fellow."

What is smaller than life in the viewfinder is much larger than life on the hanging screens—Ringer's smile and Brother Alice's.

"I will try to do my work well," Ringer says. "I will

live by the code of the People." His eyes seek out Bartholomew and look into the lens of the camera; on the viewing screens, his gaze is earnest and questioning. It reaches behind Bartholomew's mask to find his heart. Ringer is being asked to learn, Bartholomew to share what has been his exclusively. Over and over again, Bartholomew tells himself it is a good thing, that Brother Alice makes no mistakes.

"The People accept you," Brother Alice says. "The People welcome you." He takes Ringer's flesh hand in his flesh hand and the ritual is done. Bartholomew zooms in on the joining of their hands, then out again, slowly, wider and wider still, until Brother Alice and Ringer are small figures, lost among the mass of the People. He turns off the camera then, and the viewing screens go blank. Carefully, Bartholomew recaps his lens.

7

NOT SINCE SMALLNESS, when he abetted the education of the smaller still, has Bartholomew been called upon to teach, and he finds he does not much like his teacher self, who seems jealous of his expertise and of his intimacy with the tools of his craft. Ringer is young and heedless; he lacks respect for the machines and has no patience for the process of learning but expects to know everything at once, as if magic and not practice were the key to competence. Worse yet, he sheds. All over the studio, Bartholomew finds discarded straggles of Ringer's brown/blond fur. His work solitude is spoiled by an apprentice whose energy and whose questions both seem endless.

That Brother Alice had a motive in assigning Ringer to him, Bartholomew doesn't doubt; just what it is, he frequently wonders. Perhaps Brother Alice sensed that he was too attached to his work and its tools, guilty of self-importance, and needed to be humbled and taught compassion. Perhaps he has too easily forgotten the lessons of patience and sharing the small ones learn. At these times, he sees Ringer as a sort of punishment, visited on him to demonstrate his faults of spirit. On those rare occasions when Bartholomew is forbearing and allows Ringer to please him, he feels more charitably that perhaps Brother Alice intended only that he should have a helper and companion, nothing more. Ringer's mobility and strength *could* be useful, his exuberance, trimmed and trained, might be an asset.

First he must learn. They sit together in the studio, watching some tape Ringer has shot. It's obvious that Ringer is still infatuated with the powers of the camera;

the tape is so frenetic it makes Bartholomew tired and nervous just to watch it. "Restraint is important," he tells Ringer. "You should have a *reason* to zoom in or out."

"I thought I did," Ringer defends. "I thought it would be boring to stay with one shot too long."

"The camera should enhance, not distract," Bartholomew lectures. "See how distracting all your tricks are?"

Ringer nods silently, eyes sad, and Bartholomew regrets his harshness. Still, he believes what he says: everything he has to teach Ringer, he first taught himself, by trial and error, with no master but his own willingness to learn. Now he expects Ringer to forswear experiment and take his wisdom whole. He looks for something to praise in the tape. "It's in focus," he says. "You hold the camera steady."

"Do you really think so?" Ringer is resilient, so ready to be encouraged that Bartholomew softens a little.

"I do," he says. "If Brother Alice has no work for us tomorrow and the weather is good, we'll do something special." Bartholomew is thinking of birds. There is no subject better, either to develop patience or to give joy. The light in Ringer's eyes rewards him. "I'm going to see Brother Alice now," Batholomew says. "Erase the tape and put it away. Then you're free for a while. But remember tonight. Meet me here before dinner." He wheels himself toward the door, but feels a question follow him. "What is it, Ringer?"

"Nothing."

"Say it."

Ringer hesitates, then says, "Can I take the camera? Just for a little while. Just to practice."

Bartholomew looks sternly at him.

"If you don't need it," Ringer amends.

Bartholomew doesn't. He planned to edit, not to shoot, in the time before dinner. Still. Still, Ringer forgets to put the lens cap on when he isn't shooting. Bartholomew carries the camera as if it were a nestling, cradled on his lap, but Ringer flings it about as if it were an object of no importance, a toy. Everything in Bartholomew resists the loan. What if Ringer breaks it? What then?

"I'll be careful," Ringer says. "I'll remember the lens cap. I go to sleep at night chanting, *lens cap, lens cap.* I'll remember, Bartholomew."

A certain release comes with saying yes, though Bartholomew knows he will worry every minute the camera is out of his custody, in Ringer's hands. "Just for a little while," he says, then bites down on further warnings. He could waste half a day with his cautions, and still Ringer would find mistakes to make. Besides, Brother Alice is waiting. Ringer hops like a child to show his pleasure. As he bounces, his prosthetic elbow crashes against the cabinet and several music tapes tumble to the floor. Awkwardly, Ringer crouches to pick them up. Bartholomew scolds, but once outside, despite his apprehension, finds he is smiling as he rolls down the path in the pale sun.

Brother Alice appears to be doing nothing, not even thinking, when Bartholomew arrives. His smock is yellow, brighter than the sun outside, and seems to turn his silver skin to gold. "How goes the teaching?" he asks.

The question is cheerful and seems offhand, but Bartholomew feels obliged to confess his deficiencies. "I'm less patient than I should be," he says. "I ought to be more generous."

"I trust your fairness," Brother Alice says. "If you

didn't worry about your teaching, you wouldn't be a good teacher."

"With television, there are many things to think about at once. So far, Ringer thinks of some and forgets others."

Brother Alice smiles, all but the green eye smiles. Bartholomew feels it judges him.

"But he learns," Brother Alice says.

"Oh, yes. He learns."

"Then you're doing well. The Fathers have sent something for you, Bartholomew." Brother Alice rises then bends, to lift something onto the table. "If there are going to be two makers of television, then there should be two cameras." What he puts on the table is a corrugated metal case, less shinily silver than his scales.

Bartholomew stares at it and feels his flesh hand tremble.

"It's lighter than the other. You should be able to use it more easily. Open the case, Bartholomew. It's yours."

He moves close and reaches out to release the latches, slowly lifts up the lid. Inside, the camera nestles in blue velvet, the case shaped to its contours.

When he lifts his eyes, Brother Alice is smiling. "You can touch it," he says.

While Bartholomew takes the camera from its case, Brother Alice puts the recorder on the table. The camera is wonderfully light. It clings to Bartholomew's shoulder as lightly as his smock.

"Try it," Brother Alice says.

Inside the recorder, a fresh cassette awaits his images. Bartholomew connects camera to recorder, removes the lens cap and tests switches and dials until a red glow lights the edges of the viewfinder, and an image of Brother Alice appears inside the frame. He focuses, then tests the lens, longer and sharper than any he's ever used. Already the camera fits him as well as his prosthesis. Prosthetic sight, he thinks. A super-eye.

Brother Alice's smile fades in the viewfinder; his face grows grave and he leans forward, toward the camera. "How long will it take you to teach Ringer to make television?"

Reluctantly, Bartholomew detaches enough of his attention from the new machine to answer. "There's a lot to learn. And after he learns, he needs to practice. It takes time."

"Teach him quickly." Bartholomew hears command in Brother Alice's voice, and urgency. He lowers the camera to his lap. His silence is a question.

"I have other work for you, Bartholomew. Work hard with Ringer. One reason I chose him was for speed. His mind is quick, like yours."

As Brother Alice speaks, Bartholomew's flesh hand caresses the new camera. It is cool and sleek to his touch. He doesn't want new work.

"The People need television. Teach Ringer more than what you know about the machines. Teach him to see as clearly and feel as deeply as you do."

Despite the stifled feeling in his chest, Bartholomew obeys the code and promises to try. Brother Alice nods and seems satisfied, more confident of his chances for success than he is himself. Ringer *is* fast, he *does* have good ideas, but teaching—Bartholomew has thought of him as helper, not successor. To teach at all, he has had to cling to the idea of his own superiority, of the worth of his experience. Must he give away what he was so long learning, make easy for Ringer what was hard for him? This seems to be what Brother Alice asks of him and Bartholomew wonders, all the while ashamed of his doubt, if he is able or even willing to be so generous.

The new camera is a comfort, though. Its capabilities

excite him. Only in dreams has he experienced the clarity, the length and depth of vision its lens permits, only with his mind's eye seen color so vibrantly or shadows so subtle. Its zoom is smooth as cream and sweet as honey. The camera excites love in him, not the comradely love the People feel for one another, but a love that is both possessive and irrational, a desire not explained or sanctioned at the Place, to master and to merge.

It's midafternoon, and a low sun stretches out the shadows, flattens and exaggerates their distal parts. A chill in the air seems to outline every object, every leaf and rock, until the images are brittly fine.

The new camera scuttles his plans to edit and sets his course toward the gardens where what birds outlast the change of season can be found. There is a place he likes especially, a small clearing among ornamental shrubs where he can wait until the birds, startled at his arrival, forget his presence and come out of hiding. Then, hidden himself, he can shoot them. Almost to the spot, he hears something, a sound not of the place, and stops to listen. Two crows, invisible in the tall trees, argue, but it is not crows that stop him, not the chatter of swallows, but a crack and rustle, heavier and less insouciant than the skittering of birds. A larger animal? Another crack, followed by silence, a rustle. Bartholomew searches the bushes, scans the treetops without discovering the source of that foreign noise.

A laugh rings out and startles him. His grip on the camera case tightens, while his eyes seek out the origin of laughter. From his own hiding place among the shrubs, a lens peers out at him, a single mischievous eye stares him down. Then Ringer rises from his crouch and shows himself above the greenery, camera on his shoulder, a grin on his face. "Did I scare you?" he wants to know.

Bartholomew's long exhalation admits surprise. "You. What are you doing here?"

Ringer steps out of the bushes, onto the path. "I'm practicing. I thought it would be interesting to see if I could be quiet enough to make the birds trust me."

"And?"

Ringer laughs. "Every time I had a good shot, my nose started itching. Or when I reached up to take the lens cap off, I'd brush a twig and scare the birds again. I haven't got much." He looks down at Bartholomew and the silver case he clutches tightly in his lap. "What are you doing here? What's that?"

"A new camera. I was going to try it out."

"On birds?" Ringer asks, and Bartholomew nods.

8

RINGER COVERS, Bartholomew embellishes. To documentary a second camera contributes the possibility of art. Shooting a chairball match, Ringer records the action and logic of the game while Bartholomew mines detail—hands on levers, the circular blur of speeding wheels, sweat beaded on a player's brow. Later, editing, they argue zealously, in love with argument.

"Music should be the master track," Ringer says. "Edit the picture to fit the music."

"You only say that because your ear is better than your eye," Bartholomew says.

"I say it because it makes sense. The music already has continuity and rhythm."

Bartholomew says, "Pictures shouldn't become the slave of sound. That makes no sense at all."

In practice, they edit both ways. Television at the Place grows more complex, the People notice and say they like it. As Ringer gains competence, the nature of their arguments changes, slowly and progressively, from the confrontation of egos to the clash of ideas. They no longer dispute mistakes so much as methods, and for the first time Bartholomew knows the joys of talking shop. He has been so long without an educated audience that he would talk it endlessly.

The chairball game is edited, the tape rewound and filed. It has taken a long time to finish, and they plunge out of the studio into a darkness filled with winter stars.

"I still don't like the last dissolve. We should have made a straight cut." Ringer's words are a gust of white steam, ghostly in the dark.

"That would contrast the pictures, not connect them. The ball and the wheel have roundness in common."

"Their purposes are different. That's more important than form."

The argument carries them to the dwelling houses. Their rooms are in the same building on different floors. Every night, Ringer gets off the elevator on the red floor while Bartholomew rides on to green. Tonight he asks, "Would you like to come up? We could keep talking." He says it shyly. For all the time they spend together now, they have never visited each other's rooms.

Ringer agrees to come, and when the elevator stops on red, they wait together until the door closes, and rise on. Entering Bartholomew's room forestalls conversation while Ringer examines carefully each small thing that differentiates it from all other identical rooms and makes it Bartholomew's own.

For a long time he studies the photograph of a crow in flight, its body tilted against the sky so that both wings are fully visible, seen from below. He says nothing but appears to think deeply, tilting his head from time to time as if the motion freshens his thoughts. At last he says, "There's something about the birds, Bartholomew. I've noticed it often, but I don't quite understand it."

Bartholomew, too, looks at the crow.

"Something about shape," Ringer says.

Bartholomew nods. "They're the same on both sides," he says.

"All birds are the same."

"Not exactly the same," Bartholomew says.

"Their bodies are the same, though," Ringer says. "Have you ever seen a bird with just one wing?"

Bartholomew has not.

"They have two wings and two legs and two eyes. They all have feathers. They all can fly. It seems strange, Bartholomew."

Bartholomew says what he is sure by now they both are thinking. "Because the People are not the same."

"Why is that, Bartholomew?"

Bartholomew stares at the crow, at the dark symmetry of wings against the sky. "I don't know."

"Flowers, too. And trees."

"The insects," Bartholomew says. "I know."

"Where do the birds go when they leave the Place, Bartholomew? What have they seen that we can't see?"

Bartholomew shakes his head. Ringer speaks out loud questions that hover like clouds at the horizon of consciousness, questions that shape themselves in dreams and survive imperfectly when he wakes up. There is a certain relief in knowing the questions ask themselves of Ringer, too.

"Look at us, Bartholomew."

There is no mirror but the window with the night behind it. The light traps their images and gives them back. They are not the same. One stands, one-legged, while one must sit, his leg-limbs useless. One is furry, one naked of fur. Each has one arm of flesh, one hand, but even these are not the same. Their prostheses are not the same. They are similar, one form recognizes and salutes the other, but they are not the same. They turn from the window.

"Why?" Ringer says.

Bartholomew repeats the small ones' litany: "Nature is wise and keeps its secrets," but neither of them is satisfied. The words shore up the mysteries but don't explain them; the words acknowledge that there are questions but refuse to answer them.

Ringer says, "Brother Alice knows. I'm sure he does."

His eyes, more gold than brown, fix on Bartholomew, asking for more than help. "Have you ever asked him?"

Bartholomew says no. He has never asked. He has never dared to ask.

"You're closer to Brother Alice than anyone else. You see him every day. He trusts you."

"Maybe he trusts me because I don't ask questions." Ringer's eyes follow even when he averts his own.

"Don't you want to know?" Ringer asks.

On the surface, the question seems reasonable and fair, but in the pit of Bartholomew's stomach, it feels like heresy. Does he really want to know the answers? Will answers make him happier or better than he is? No, something deep and orthodox inside him warns. No. The wisdom of the Place is self-contained. It is a circle, and a circle is a perfect form. To break it would be dangerous.

"Nature is endlessly creative," Bartholomew says. "We are its medium." He looks at Ringer. "That's what I sometimes think."

"We learn to be fair," Ringer says, "but Nature isn't fair. Some of the People suffer the slow death, while others die easily. Some of the People can't see. Some can't hear. Some can't walk."

"The blind ones hear better than those who see," Bartholomew says. "And those who can't hear use their fingers to speak and their eyes to listen. Maybe," he says, "Nature is still experimenting. Maybe we're all experiments."

"Nature is stupid, then," Ringer says. "Are you willing to admit that Nature is stupid? If something is good, if it works well, we repeat it. We learn. Why doesn't Nature learn, Bartholomew?"

Ringer's face is fierce inside its frame of fur, and the smooth curve of his forehead is disrupted by thought.

"Maybe," Bartholomew says, "maybe we're too stupid to understand what Nature learns."

Ringer sits on Bartholomew's bed and his fingers pluck idly at the blankets. His voice is low. "I'll tell you something, Bartholomew. I didn't expect to be a maker of television. Before I came of age, I wanted to be an inventor. I made things, tools and toys, for my friends. I expected to be Boris's apprentice, not yours."

It has never occurred to Bartholomew that Ringer might be discontent as his apprentice. "Are you unhappy?" he asks.

Ringer answers slowly. "Not now. Not anymore."

"At first."

"Yes. Until I saw that television requires invention, I was unhappy."

"So Brother Alice was wise."

"I wonder." Ringer's voice is almost a whisper. "I think Brother Alice didn't want me to be an inventor, Bartholomew. If I was an inventor, if I was Nature, I would give all the People two eyes and two arms and two legs."

"Legs aren't so important, Ringer. My chair carries me where I need to go."

"Wouldn't you rather have legs than not?" Ringer asks.

In his dreams sometimes, Bartholomew has legs. He can't see them, he can't see himself at all in dreaming, but he feels that he's running, putting his feet on the earth and pushing against its firmness. Past the houses, past the gardens, he runs. He loves to run. Sometimes, of course, he has wings, too, and flies. "I don't think about it," he tells Ringer. " 'I accept myself, I accept my brother.' That's what we learn as small ones."

"Sometimes," says Ringer, "I think the wisdom means to keep us small."

Bartholomew wonders. If this is true, it too is wise. The small ones are happy, the world in smallness is big enough to accommodate all dreams. "The wisdom means to keep us happy," he says. What was meant as statement comes out a question. To make a sentence is to hypothesize. Not for the first time, Bartholomew wishes all wisdom could be visual. He trusts the testimony of his eyes above the pretty experiments his tongue makes.

Aloud, to Ringer, he says, "All thought is testing."

9

THERE ARE TWO DEATHS AT THE PLACE. One is a long, slow battle waged within the body, for the body. An alien invades. With terrible persistence, its armies attack, colonize and consume the well-organized bureaucracy of organs and tissue and bone. The war can be long, but the outcome is never in doubt. In time, every time, the duly established government is overthrown, the barbarian always wins and, in winning, becomes self-defeating: with the victim, the victor dies. The People call this death the Sickness. By its vicissitudes, the spirit is driven from the body.

In the second kind of death, the eviction of soul from substance is accomplished quickly and almost without pain. The heart stops. The brain asphyxiates, the organs starve, the spirit departs an empty house.

The Fathers do not disrupt this process. They do not forestall it. They know that in the bodies of the People, both deaths coexist, at the heart of their constituent cells, both deaths inhere and that the choice between them is made by time, by circumstance and at least in part by temperament. Accident has no time to befall the People. It is written in their genes they shall die young.

10

"I MUST GO TO THE FATHERS, Bartholomew,"
Brother Alice says. "And you must learn to do my work
when I'm gone."

The words incite a deep and cruel pain. Spontane-
ously, Bartholomew's eyes fill with tears. Before the
first of these can fall, Brother Alice laughs, and Bartholomew feels his laughter as a second hurt.

"You misunderstood," Brother Alice says. "I'm sorry.
I'm going to visit the Fathers, not to stay with them. I
have no intention of dying."

"I'm glad," Bartholomew says. He says it simply, his
words have all the weight of utter honesty, and Brother
Alice laughs again. Again, the laughter hurts. His response, goodwilling though it was, was somehow inap-
propriate. That his deepest feelings should cause
amusement stings and humbles him. In his mind, Bartholomew hears Ringer's voice, claiming the moment
as a point in favor of his thesis: that the Fathers do not
trust them with the truth; that the Fathers look at the
People as at children, with amusement and disdain.
Ringer would ask questions now, and several questions
frame themselves in Bartholomew's mind, but they do
so without urgency, and he forbears to ask them, only
waits for Brother Alice to go on.

Again, he apologizes. "I didn't mean to belittle your
feelings, Bartholomew. I'm flattered that you'd grieve
for me."

That he would grieve, the potential of his grief, hangs
between them, and seems to Bartholomew to be a further proof of his insufficiency. It is safer to say nothing
than to risk the silver laughter that lacks of joy.

"You have too much to learn to waste time on sadness," Brother Alice says, and Bartholomew thinks again of Ringer, who wants answers and would gladly learn new work. Even now, without a camera, he frames the scene—Brother Alice, living, in the foreground, and beyond his shoulder, looking down, the painted Brother Alice hung on the wall.

The subject disrupts the shot by rising, he walks briskly, he presses a button and despite confusion and amazement, Bartholomew tracks the action, he covers the event. The wall of Brother Alice's room slides back into itself and disappears. Brother Alice crosses an invisible threshold and turns to summon him. It takes Bartholomew a moment to understand that he is meant to be an actor in this play, that he must follow and react, not just record.

"Come," Brother Alice says again.

He comes. The wall slides shut behind him, and he pans the new space, a long, low room with white walls, full of machines he does not recognize. The sight of a television set anchors his senses and he stares for a moment at the blank and unlit screen.

A circle hangs against the wall. Two raised black lines join at the origin and point outward, toward the circumference, drawing radial cords on the white face. As he studies the circle, one of the lines moves forward, only a small distance, with a muted mechanical *brrr*.

Brother Alice stands beside Bartholomew. He points to the circle. "It's called a clock," he says. "The Fathers use it to measure time."

As Bartholomew watches, the clock makes its nervous sound and again the black line advances, a distance equal to the first jump. "I don't understand," he says.

"The Fathers' time is very crowded. They give it

names to help them use it well." Brother Alice produces a small plastic box. Under a clear dome, there is another circle, smaller than the one on the wall, its rim fringed with short black lines. "Already you can count to ten," Brother Alice says, "but the Fathers give names to numbers beyond ten. You'll have to learn those names. Count with me now."

While they count in unison, Brother Alice points in turn to each of ten figures on the face of the circle. When Bartholomew stops, as he must, at ten, Brother Alice names on, ". . . eleven, twelve. Can you say the numbers now?" He hands the clock to Bartholomew, who points and names.

"Very good, Bartholomew," and Bartholomew has a moment's pleasure at his success before Brother Alice tells him the lesson is not done. He produces another circle, larger than the one on the wall, so that each of the short black lines marking the circumference is clearly visible.

Pointing, they count to sixty once, once more, again. Bartholomew learns that each quarter of the clock has fifteen lines, that four times fifteen makes sixty lines, a circle. His memory is good, and he learns the names of the numbers quickly. He cannot imagine their utility.

Brother Alice fixes two black arms to the face of the larger circle and moves them slowly around it, marking hours and the pieces of hours called minutes. Bartholomew is at ease with machines and doesn't fear the mechanism, but he fails to understand why the Fathers feel the need to measure time so carefully. To measure time takes time. It distracts from doing, and Bartholomew would rather be doing now, making television with machines whose purpose is obvious and makes sense to him.

Brother Alice arranges the black arms in different

positions and asks Bartholomew to tell the time. At first he is often wrong, but after many repetitions, his accuracy improves. Brother Alice explains that two complete trips of the shorter arm around the dial is equal to one day and one night, from dawn to dawn, but that the numbers themselves don't correspond directly with the cycles of the sun.

"Why not?" Bartholomew asks, and Brother Alice thinks for a moment before he says it is one of the mysteries. By the end of the lesson, Bartholomew has learned enough to see that the clock's longer arm has traveled three circles, and the shorter one advanced three times. It is six o'clock. This has little meaning to him until Brother Alice says, "The dinner bell will ring now," and it does.

The birds fly round and round an invariable circle that is and is not the sun. The circle is unchanging because the birds are leashed by long cords to the point that is the circle's center. Sometimes they fly slowly, and Bartholomew is amazed at their ability to fly upside down, on their backs, as they trace the lower portion of the sphere. Sometimes they fly dizzyingly fast, so that the motion of their flight lingers on his retina, until the whole circumference is darkened by a second, abiding circle, motion made visible by speed. When the intercom first calls him, he imagines it is the birds who speak his name, soft but commandingly. He cannot tell what they want, unless it is to be free of their bonds and of the circle.

Bartholomew! Bartholomew!

Bartholomew would help them if he could.

The voice persists, and now Bartholomew knows it is Brother Alice who calls him.

The bright light of the office hurts his eyes after the starless, moonless night outside. When Brother Alice, hurtfully resplendent, says the outsiders are coming soon and he must meet them, Bartholomew accepts the news as if in dreaming, with no expectations and no surprise. When the strangers arrive, minutes later, they resemble creatures of dream—two of them, tall and hooded, wrapped in black cloaks that hide their bodies. At first, he assumes they are twins, but with time sees that their white faces, while similar, are not identical. One is round and one rectangular. The one named William smiles more deeply and easily than the one Brother Alice calls Fritz, who barely speaks or smiles at all. Their hands, extending to him, are gloved in black leather. Large goggles with yellow plastic lenses conceal their eyes.

"William fixes what is broken," Brother Alice tells him, "and Fritz brings us what we need." Brother Alice goes on to order food for the kitchens, bleach for the laundry, clay for the potters, toilet paper and thread and medicines. To William he gives the tasks of fixing a leaking faucet in the poolhouse and a light in the elevator of one of the dwellings. The outsiders recite their orders back to Brother Alice, and he nods. Before Bartholomew can finish his own mental recapitulation of the items, the two are leaving, as they entered, by the door that has no knob. Fritz inserts his key, turns it, draws the door open while William bids them good night. "Alice, Bartholomew, I'll see you later."

"Good night, William. Thank you," Brother Alice says, and in the seconds before the door closes, Bartholomew has a tantalizing glimpse of the world beyond, patterned intensities of light at play on a polygonal stretch of white wall. He stretches his vision, tries to look around corners and through walls, to extend his perception of the mysterious space by just one centimeter, but the door does close, shrinking the polygon smaller and smaller before it swallows it.

"That door leads to the Fathers," Brother Alice says gently. "You won't have the key." His words seal off possibility as surely as the closing of the door.

"I don't mind," Bartholomew says, feeling that he shouldn't mind and finding that, fleetingly, he does.

Brother Alice watches closely, a modicum of disbelief in his smile. "And I'm sure I don't have to tell you, these things are secrets."

Obediently, Bartholomew nods. Of course.

"The secrets will make you lonely for a while, I know. But once I return, the information can be erased from your memory tape. Your innocence can be restored."

Though Brother Alice says "can," Bartholomew understands that he means "will." He understands that he has no choice in the matter. To have no choice both comforts and insults him.

A faint smile lifts Brother Alice's red-in-silver lips. "Be glad. Ignorance is a gift," he says, and Bartholomew understands, too, that while Brother Alice talks to him it is really about himself. His understanding is that of dreams, a conviction of truth snared perfectly in paradox, and he feels no need to question it. Instead he says, "I'm sorry that you're lonely." Spoken, his words strike him as bold and impudent. He watches Brother Alice's blue eye change, reflective as his scales in sunlight. Finally, Brother Alice laughs. "I don't know what to do with your sympathy," he says, and he seems genuinely perplexed.

"Accept it," Bartholomew dares to advise.

Abruptly, Brother Alice rises from his chair. "It's I who should be sorry. I know you don't like power. On the other hand, that's why I trust you with it." He turns to Bartholomew, his flesh hand spread, palm up, in supplication, but Bartholomew can't guess what he is asking for. Talking to Brother Alice often wearies him. The People say what they mean, simply and directly, their meanings reside in their words, but when Brother Alice speaks, he seems to say less than he means and to intend much more.

Bartholomew says all he is capable of meaning: "I'll try to do my best."

Among the People, it is a nearly ritual response. It means that one accepts responsibility and is absolved of failure. Brother Alice seems dissatisfied with it. His green eye grants no absolution, his blue eye probes until Bartholomew feels his very nervous system is exposed, raw and susceptible, to its gaze. Brother Alice's power has never been more palpable, and to Bartholomew it seems a fearsome thing, capable of damaging both he who wields it and him on whom its force is turned. The air feels electric; his synapses crackle. Brother Alice's face grows large, approaching his, each shining silver scale appears discrete, and for the first time, Bartholomew perceives the pattern of their overlapping. It is a zoom performed without his agency and doesn't stop until Brother Alice's lips are pressed against his lips, until he can feel breath soft on his cheek and the brush of silver scales against his neck. For the term of this contact, he does not breathe and his blood feels busy under his skin. So close, his eyes lose resolution and he shuts them, retreats into a blackness slashed by luminescence. Somewhere, something sings, a fast, high-pitched melody, and the voice reminds him of his own.

As he would not approach Brother Alice, so he will not retreat. The embrace persists, unmoving, and Bartholomew imagines the few small places their bodies touch radiate a heat that must be visible as light. Brother Alice pulls away from him, and Bartholomew feels the separation as coldness on his skin. When he opens his eyes, he finds Brother Alice has not retreated far, but looks intently at him. "Now you have something to forgive me," Brother Alice says.

Bartholomew cannot imagine forces as elemental as heat and light burdened with moral weight, but he is willing to forgive if form demands it. Brother Alice's high green eye remains aloof, but the lively shining blue one joins gaze with his eyes, and doesn't waver when he says, "Whatever you ask me, I will do."

Brother Alice nods, accepting this. "I know," he says.

11

HIS FINGERS ITCH to play the buttons of the editing console, and his shoulder aches for the weight of the camera more sharply than he's ever mourned not having legs. Slowly, he conjures a smile up out of emptiness and says, "It's very good. I like it."

Ringer touches a button and the tape begins to rewind. His grin is wide, and beyond the flush of pleasure at his praise, Bartholomew can see the deeper glow of pride that makes his praise irrelevant. "I like it, too," Ringer says. "I liked making it." After a moment's pause, he adds, "I missed your help, of course."

His words are more kind than true, but Bartholomew finds another smile inside himself and puts it on. "Of course." The truth is, the tape is different from the one he would have made and maybe—no, definitely—better. The studio has been slightly, subtly rearranged in his absence: the music tapes are closer to the console than they were, and the cameras stored higher than he, from his chair, can reach. The truth is, the apprentice has surpassed his master.

Ringer picks up another cassette. "I've even learned to shoot the birds, Bartholomew. Want to see them?"

"I'd like to, but I can't." A clock ticks in him; the Fathers' time becomes his own. He reverses the wheels of his chair and moves toward the door. "I only came to tell you the new tapes have arrived. Ernest will bring them later."

Ringer raises his hand in a mock salute. "Brother Bartholomew is wise," he says. Before Bartholomew's chair is out the door, Ringer is back at work, bent intently over the console.

The kitchens are busy. Apprentices chop and dice and grind, while Louis shuttles between huge pots on his big stove, spicing and stirring, occasionally stopping long enough to taste. "Bartholomew!" he calls. "We've just run out of peas. We need flour and lemons and bay leaves and caraway seeds, brown sugar, beets . . ." The list is long, and Bartholomew has to repeat it several times before he's sure he will remember it. As they talk, the dishwashers swish and moan continuously, like a tape played slowly backward.

Louis stoops to open the oven door, and a blast of yeasty warmth, the slightly astringent smell of new bread escapes it. A score of perfect loaves nestles inside, and Louis draws one out, then signals an apprentice to finish the unloading. He tips the loaf from its pan, with butter glazes the brown crust until it shines, then salts it lightly. "Wait until you taste this, Bartholomew." When Louis slices the bread, the loaf emits a little breath of steam. A slab of butter, melting, turns the slice a porous gold. Louis holds it out to him.

Bartholomew hesitates. The space under his tongue grows wet, anticipating the taste of the bread, its perfume signals his stomach to make room, and yet he feels he should not take it. No one at the Place gets food between the common mealtimes—it is a privilege that comes with wearing Brother Alice's shoes. Louis laughs at his reticence. "Eat," he says, "or you'll offend me."

His teeth cut a crescent from the slice, its tastes and textures dance on his tongue, but his stomach, receiving the morsel, feels hollow. He is an imposter. His authority, and the privilege that comes with it, are assumed, not earned.

"Well?" Louis asks.

Well? Any tongue at the Place could taste it as well, anyone tasting it would say it was delicious, but it's

Bartholomew's opinion Louis wants, his praise that becomes important. There is laughter in Louis's eyes, the mobile side of his face lifts in a smile, but he stands sternly expectant, demanding judgment.

Bartholomew takes another bite, a small one, and then gives in to Louis's game and to the masquerade of power. "It's perfect," he says. "As always." Louis is satisfied, and lets him go.

Outside, the sky is white, and the whiteness is greedy, devouring color until the Place, the trees and grass and buildings, seem to exist only in black and white. The wind is brisk and colder than the day. Inside himself, Bartholomew searches for color, and for warmth.

At the nursery, he does the dutiful and painful first, learning from Brutus what the nurses and the doctors need, then visiting Joseph in the bed from which he can no longer rise. Bartholomew raises the bed's head to lift the child's, and Joseph greets him happily if weakly. His joints are huge knots tied in the thin cord of his bones and his face is ancient, though he is not old, the skin taut and deeply creased over his hairless skull, his eyes and ears and nose enormous.

"I have a treat for you," Bartholomew tells him. "Guess what it is."

"A game," Joseph says.

"No."

"Music."

"No."

"A picture."

Bartholomew shakes his head. The predictable choices seem exhausted, and Joseph thinks hard before he says, "You've found a way to make me well."

Bartholomew looks away from the round, hopeful eyes and fishes in his pocket for the small packet. He gives it to the child. "Only bread, fresh from the ovens. I think it's still warm."

The child is resilient, and the bread more tangible than a cure. Joseph's teeth are loose and his gums tender, but he eats the bread with enthusiasm, one tiny bite at a time. When he's done, Bartholomew wheels himself close to the bed and wipes away a few crumbs that linger on the small pointed chin. "Don't tell the others," he warns. "The treat was just for you."

"Tell me a story, Barmew," Joseph pleads, but Bartholomew, lashed to the clock, says no. "Maybe tomorrow, Joseph. You be good."

"I always am," the child says in good-bye.

At last, Bartholomew allows himself to partake of his own pleasure. The nursery is always warm and full of life, and he is always welcome there. The small ones help care for the nestlings now, they watch and teach and bathe, they change soiled diapers and hold the nestlings patiently as they suck their bottles dry and drift to sleep. When Bartholomew arrives, they crowd around his chair, all talking and tugging on his smock at once. Ethel laughed for the first time last night, Barmew. Desdemona has a new tooth and I, I slept straight through the night last night and didn't wet my bed. Someone plops the baby Hanford in his lap. Can I push your chair, Barmew? Do you want to hear my song?

The currency of the nursery is touch, and Bartholomew spends freely, hugging and tickling and tousling hair. "The code says we should respect each other," the small ones cry. "The code says that we mustn't feed ourselves until we see that all the limbless ones have somebody to feed them. The code says that every person's work is good, and none is better than any other." The small ones recite their lessons, and he listens gravely, rewarding them with small caresses. Here life is simple and benign. He wishes he could spend the whole day with them. Amid the shrieks and giggles, impervious to the endless high-pitched chatter, Hanford has fallen asleep on his lap, and Bartholomew can see the tracery of blue veins in his pale eyelids and the slight rise of his little chest. With one flesh fingertip, he strokes the soft cheek of the sleeping infant, and for a moment he, like Ringer, curses the Fathers, that all the children should not have arms or legs or eyes that see or wings, enabling them to fly.

It is hard to say good-bye to the small ones, but the Fathers' clock insists, and he does so, sad to leave, already longing for the next day's interlude. When he lifts the tiny Hanford into a nurse's waiting arms, the baby wakes enough to cry at the separation. As he wheels himself down the nursery ramp, Bartholomew finds himself repeating again his imprecation, vaguely addressed, that the problems of the Place will stay small and easy to solve until Brother Alice returns.

The last stop of the morning is Clotho's studio. Lucas stands grandly at its center, weaving a tale with his great voice, while all the artists of the Place gather around him, trying to capture his cylindrical shape with their brushes, trying to mix a blue that matches his. Bartholomew visits each easel, amazed at how various the representations of a single subject can be, and when the artists urge him to pick a favorite among their pictures, he laughingly declines. "I like them all," he says, "but best of all, I like the model."

"You begin to sound like Brother Alice," someone observes, and another says, "He is."

"Is there anything you need?" Bartholomew asks Clotho.

"Only white," Clotho says. "We're almost out of white."

"Today you could steal it from the sky," Bartholomew says, and all the artists laugh.

"Very good, Bartholomew," Lucas booms, and as soon as he resumes his storytelling, a new character enters the tale, a painter who extracts his colors from the weather, and from the earth.

When he has finished his morning round, Bartholomew is tired and feels lonely. There is still a little time before lunch, and instead of returning to Brother Alice's empty office, he gives himself permission to visit the gardens. He hungers for the sight of birds, he wants to hear the leaves whisper around him and to sit so still the birds accept him as a shrub. He wants the birds to land on his limbs and mistake his eyes for berries. In this cold dry space between seasons, few birds remain. No snow has fallen yet, but the ducks and geese and hummingbirds are gone, while Bartholomew, bound to his clock and trapped inside, has missed their going, the shape and sound of their flight. A few crows and sparrows are the most he hopes to find as he wheels himself into his blind between bushes, birds as ordinary and steadfast as he is himself.

The white sky is birdless above him and the wind's small dirge the only song he hears. Deeply he breathes and listens closely inside himself for his own heartbeat, for the clock that keeps his body's time. Eyes closed, he tries to clean his mind of images and of the voices that would tell him he should not be sitting here, that he is a thief of time, or that the Fathers know of and will punish the theft. He breathes and does not mark his breaths with numbers, only in-out, in-out, until he hears the hum of blood in his ears and the inside of his mind is a uniform, cool gray, unmarked by shadows. He waits for birds, but does not name his waiting.

In . . . . out . . . . in . . . . out. In equal measure. Flashes of red stab at the grayness, but he dispels them, washing them away with air, with an absence of desire. In . . . . . out . . . . . in . . . . . out. The capacity of his lungs increases, the whole of his being is a bellows, admitting and expelling air. The grayness settles on his limbs and he no longer feels them. In . . . . out. He hears a low moan and believes it is his own voice, his sadness speaking in a wordless voice. The moan is soft, less a sound of complaint than of the acceptance of sorrow. It does not ask for pity or inspire it. It is the sound of seasons passing, of the inevitability of loss, of the pain of being sentient and fear of losing sensibility. What tells Bartholomew the voice is not of him is that it stops, does not respect his rhythms but simply stops, permitting silence.

His eyes open, his breathing shallows and he hears the wind. Listens, embodied now, with tension in his body. The moan comes again, is fainter. Waits . . . two, three, four. The source is very near him. He moves his chair from the blind and circles the bushes slowly. The voice cries again, and this time, he knows it calls to him.

On the ground, which is black and dry, half hidden in the tangle of oldest, lowest branches, bare of leaves, a crow rests, wings pulled tight against its body, impersonating a black stone. The crow's head inclines toward one shoulder, the black dot of an eye regards him and shares its knowledge: *I am dying. It is my time to die.* The moan now is almost beyond hearing, a soft deep sound free both of anger and of pain. It is too late to speak or intervene. Bartholomew is chosen witness and he watches the death, silent and simple and wholly terrifying. The last breath is released, the bird-heart stops its beating, the film of a lid closing hides the round eye, the black head slumps to rest against the wing, and Bartholomew breathes slowly, without moving, and binds his mind to blankness. If a spirit leaves, he does not see or hear or feel it go. If he has a soul himself, it does not stir. The death of the crow defeats the Fathers' time.

At last the lunch bell rings, and it almost surprises him to find he is alive, his body capable of hunger and of obedience to bells. His hands fly automatically to the controls of his chair, automatically he leaves the garden and steers toward the dining hall, looking back only once to the still black form, mostly obscured by branches. The great room is warm and full of people talking, laughing, eating, all oblivious to death, and what separates him from them, what makes him lonely in their company is his awareness that they each and all must die.

The simple task of picking a place at one of the big curved tables seems hard and he sits in his chair by the door, sits until he sees a hand is waving at him and that the hand belongs to Leda. The wave is an invitation. Gratefully he accepts it, maneuvers his chair into the empty space beside Leda's and, warmed slightly by his friend's welcome, begins the long journey back to forgetfulness of death. At first, he can barely taste his food, but in time, the savor seduces him and he eats hungrily. At first he has little to say beyond the formulaic, but soon the food animates him and loosens his tongue, and he finds himself telling Leda about the crow. In telling, the story becomes funny.

"What could it be? I asked myself. A hungry nestling? Maybe some new kind of animal I'd never seen before.

I looked and looked for the marvelous creature, and you know what I found? A crow. An ordinary crow."

Leda laughs appreciatively. Bartholomew knows he alters the truth—nowhere in his story do the wonder or fear of death appear; he does not mention the stunning resignation of the crow. While the sequence as he relates it is accurate enough, the tone is false—but he excuses the corruption, feeling it is better to risk falsehood courting laughter than to perpetuate despair by fidelity to truth. Tears of laughter well up in Leda's eyes, and he takes and squeezes Bartholomew's hand. By the end of the meal, he no longer feels sad, but only tired, as if he'd lived several days in half of one. Leda's company is so soothing, in fact, so pleasant, that Bartholomew invites him to come back to the office and help him pass the afternoon.

Again, Leda laughs. "You must think I have nothing to do with *my* days. I've made up a new dance, and after lunch we practice it. Today, Ringer's going to tape us so we can see ourselves and how the dance looks. Then we'll be able to make changes and corrections before we perform it for the People when Peter comes of age."

Bartholomew should be pleased, he commands himself to be pleased, but somehow it hurts him that Ringer will see Leda's dance before he does. Bartholomew has taped all of Leda's dances. He has no word for jealousy, but feels it in his stomach, as a weight at the corners of his smile.

"You could come and watch, too," Leda tells him.

Bartholomew shakes his head. "I couldn't. I promised Brother Alice to be in his office every afternoon, in case the People want to bring me their problems."

Leda's teeth are white when he smiles. "What you gain in importance, you lose in pleasure," Leda says.

"No one comes to me with problems," Bartholomew says. "Either the People don't have any problems, or they know I'm too stupid to help them."

"It's not that, Bartholomew. The People think you're too busy now to listen to their troubles."

"I can't even solve my own problems," Bartholomew says. "And one of my problems is loneliness. I sit alone all afternoon."

"So come to the poolhouse and watch the dance."

"I can't," Bartholomew says. "I promised to stay in the office."

The office, as usual, is empty and he, as usual, is bored. To pass the time, he wheels himself around the room, near the walls, trying to square his corners as precisely as possible, he tries to make up stories to explain the pictures on the walls, he looks at the portrait of Brother Alice and wishes he were here. He wishes he had a camera now and could make television. If he had a camera, he would make a tape that was all white walls and square corners and his tape would show the People what it is to be bored. The only sound he would put on the track would be the sound of wheels rocking back and forth, and the voice of a lonely person talking out loud to himself just to make sure his voice still works. He is doing just this, saying "Bartholomew is lonely," when the door opens and a young one hops in on his crutch. Bartholomew has seen him often and noted the redness of his hair, but doesn't know his name.

"Are you busy?" the young one asks.

Bartholomew smiles. "I was busy waiting for you."

The young one assumes he speaks seriously. "Then you must know what I want to say."

"No," Bartholomew says. "All I know is that I'm glad you've come. Sit down."

The young one approaches the chair with energy,

almost attacks it. He moves deftly, well adapted to the body that he has—one full leg and one half, one full arm and one several inches shorter that has no usual hand, no opposable thumb but—Bartholomew counts them—seven well-developed fingers. His eyes are yellow/green.

"Tell me your name," Bartholomew says.

"My name is Peter."

Bartholomew remembers. "You're going to come of age soon."

"The doctors expect me tomorrow night."

"That's good. Soon we will welcome you."

Peter drops his eyes to watch the flexing of his seven fingers. Bartholomew sees they grow not in a line but in a circle and can touch each other, tip to tip. "I'm not ready," Peter says.

"Why not?"

"I'm afraid," the young one says. In his eyes, or in the flesh around them, worry underlines his words.

"Afraid of what?" Bartholomew asks. "Not of work, surely." Peter's work is not yet chosen. It is something he must discuss with Brother Alice.

"Not of work. Not if my work is music."

Glad of the clue, Bartholomew nods. "Tell me about your music."

"When I was small," Peter says, "Boris made me an instrument. It has both strings and stops." He raises his shorter arm and wiggles the congery of fingers. "Nobody can play it but me."

"I'd like to hear you play it."

"If the doctors change my hand, I won't be able to. All my music will be lost."

Bartholomew is used to clinging to the good. "You could learn to play a different instrument," he says, but Peter shakes his head in vehement refusal. "This is my hand. I've trained it to serve me, and I don't want metal in its place."

The passion in his voice makes Bartholomew share his concern. He ponders Peter's problem, then says, "Maybe the doctors plan to leave you your hand." He glances downward at his own weak and truncated lower limbs. "Sometimes there's nothing else they can do."

"Zelda's hand was like mine before he came of age. Now he has metal."

"What can your fingers do besides play music?" Bartholomew asks.

"Lots of things," Peter says proudly. "I can grip and carry. My fingers are strong. And the small ones like to play with them. They paint faces on them and I move them and we pretend they're people."

"You want a second leg?" Bartholomew asks. He stalls with questions while he waits for wisdom. There is no assurance it will come to him.

"I'd like a leg, yes," Peter says. "And I'd like you to talk to the doctors. Can you do that, Bartholomew?"

"I don't know," he says. No wisdom, but an idea comes to him. "Go get your instrument," he says, "and play it for me. If the dinner bell rings, ignore it. Louis will give us food later."

When Peter's gone to fetch his instrument, Bartholomew calls Ringer on the intercom. Minutes later, he appears at the office with camera and recorder and sets them up. Peter's instrument, when he brings it, is a hybrid of flute and lute, a slim woodwind body married to a smooth acoustic bulge strung with eight strings for Peter's seven fingers to pluck and strum. The whole creation hangs around his neck on a leather strap. When he plays, his music speaks with two voices, but it doesn't sound like two people playing two instruments:

there is no conflict, only harmony. The instrument and its sound remind Bartholomew of his own body, of how, in the Excitement, his two parts converse, of how two feelings, subtly different, exist as one. Peter's music excites him, and he listens hard.

As he listens, he watches Ringer shoot, how he explores first the flute hand, then the lute hand with his lens. Both occupy the frame at once. To study one above the other is a matter of changing focus, and Ringer does so smoothly and surely, in response to the music itself. After Peter has played several pieces of his own composing, Bartholomew signals him to stop. "This tape is for the doctors," he says. "I hope it will show them that your hand is not a problem but a gift."

Untimely creases leave Peter's brow and he grins happily, too hopefully. The dinner bell rings and Bartholomew gives him permission to go. Peter waves his many fingers and hops away. Ringer tarries, packing his equipment slowly. He looks up at Bartholomew. "Do you really think you can convince the doctors to leave his hand alone?" he asks.

Bartholomew returns his gaze, caught between temptations. He would like to share his anxiety and tell the truth—that he has no idea if it is even possible to speak to the doctors, much less influence them, but he is reluctant for Ringer, Ringer who shoots Leda's new dance, to know he is so powerless. He answers evasively. "We'll see," he says.

Watching television after dinner exhausts him. His craftsman's knowledge deprives him of the simple pleasures of spectation, and he can't accept the thing as made but remakes every choice, every decision already made. Watching is working: he reshoots, he re-edits, asks different questions of the subject, cuts to different music, uses a fade here instead of a dissolve, a jump cut there and at the end, has nothing to show for his effort but mild indigestion, fed by envy and unrequited love. Though dark comes early now, while the People still eat their dinner, it's not late when the evening's telecast is over; downstairs in the common rooms, people play games or make music together and in the rooms around his, he can hear a low melody of smaller, more intimate conversations, lyrics inaudible; he knows that Leda is swimming, most likely, and Clotho is in his studio, mining a few more productive hours from the day, but reticence and weariness combine to keep him from seeking company. Instead, he puts himself provisionally to bed, still dressed and ready to serve if called upon, but half withdrawn from service, too, and counts the small holes gridded on the noise-absorbing ceiling tile until he sleeps.

When he awakes it is deep night and it is fear that wakes him, fear that he's failed to keep his rendezvous with the messengers, that the phone has rung and rung in the empty secret office until Brother Alice, among the Fathers, recognized his dereliction and gave him up. Remorse makes him hurry, getting up, and haste makes him clumsy. It seems to take forever to work the sling of the derrick around his buttocks and when it's fast, and he directs himself through the darkness to where his chair should be, he finds it missing. With his flippers he combs the darkness, all the while suspended uncertainly in air, and for the moment, uncharitably, is willing to believe that someone, wanting to hurt or humble him, has moved his chair while he slept. The sensation is so nightmarish that he tries to wake himself, struggles psychically to deny his dilemma, but it persists. Absurdity *is* reality. The part of his mind bound to his body, swinging precariously in darkness, is pushed toward tears, while the watcher part who escapes his body is free to look and laugh at his predicament.

At last his flippers brush against something more substantial than air, he finds his chair and drops himself ungently in it. He enters the office, breathless, just as William is arriving. The clock says they both are late.

"Sorry," William says. "I got hung up at home."

"Me, too," Bartholomew tells him. "Tonight there's nothing that needs fixing. You're free to go."

William, settled on a chair, stays on. "Fritz is sick. Couldn't make it tonight. If you tell me what you need, I'll pass it on."

Bartholomew opens his mouth to recite the list but finds he can't remember it. He can picture himself in the kitchens, repeating to Louis, he remembers assuring the nurses their needs would be filled, but when he tries to call up what they wanted, his mind is vengefully blank. Digitoxin? That was yesterday. Yesterday, Louis asked for pineapple and beans. Toilet paper. Cleansing powder. Toothpaste.

"Well?" William says.

"I can't remember."

William laughs.

Bartholomew is sick with self-recrimination. Guilty of truancy and self-absorption. "I've failed the People," he says miserably.

William doesn't temper his smile. "Hey, it's all right," he says kindly. "Everybody makes mistakes sometimes."

"Brother Alice doesn't make mistakes. It was my work to remember."

"Once," William says, "I spent a whole night trying to fix the generator when it was the refrigeration plant that was on the blink."

Instead of laughing, Bartholomew begins to cry. William watches for a moment, his eyes inscrutable behind the yellow goggles, lips flat with disbelief, before he grins and says, "Hey, so the cabbage is a day late. So what. It's not the end of the world."

"I'm unworthy."

"I think you're blowing this thing way out of proportion," William tells him. "Listen. I forgot our anniversary once. That's ten times bigger than the shopping list, but Darlene got over it." In face of Bartholomew's disconsolate silence, he goes on. "You want to know a secret? Fritz isn't really sick. He just wanted a night off. He said he had a date, so I'm covering for him. I won't tell Alice if you won't."

The idea of concealing anything from Brother Alice, of failing to confess himself is so novel to Bartholomew that it shocks him out of tears. He stares dry-eyed at William, who rises now, with a rustle of his long black cape. "There now," he says. "Is that all that was eating you? Hell, you can trust me, Bartholomew. I won't tell." At the door, he turns back. "Chin up, fella. I'll see you tomorrow night."

When the door shuts behind William, Bartholomew touches his chin, then pushes it upward. It fails to lift his spirits. The phone rings then, and when he answers, Brother Alice is with him. Despite guilt, the sweet voice is restorative. "Do you have problems you need to share with me?" he asks.

Bartholomew tells him about Peter. At first his story is flat and tentative, but by the end, he's eloquent. "No one else can make music like his. Maybe his seven fingers are a special gift."

"What do you think?" Brother Alice asks. "Do you think he should be allowed to keep his hand as it is?"

Bartholomew says yes without hesitation.

"Then I'll speak to the doctors. I trust your judgment. Take the tape you made to the nursery and leave it with Brutus, so the doctors can see it when they come. Is that all?"

Brother Alice's voice sounds tired, with a plod in place of the usual lilt, and Bartholomew decides to keep the news of his failure to himself. Still, he is unwilling to break the connection. "How are the Fathers?" he presumes to inquire.

Brother Alice sighs. "Oh, contentious. As usual."

Bartholomew has no answer to a word he doesn't know.

"That means they argue a lot about what's best for the People."

"Oh," Bartholomew says. Then: "But you could tell them."

"I think so, too, Bartholomew. If only they'd listen." Another sigh. "I have to get some sleep now, and so should you. Good night," Brother Alice says.

The line clicks, then buzzes. Bartholomew holds the receiver for a few seconds, then, even though it no longer connects him to Brother Alice, replaces it almost reverently in its cradle. "Good night," he says.

12

UP, UP SHE RISES. When she reenters her body (has she really been gone?) she finds her skin is damp, her pulse fast, limbs languid. A scent both sweet and salty hovers in the darkness above her bed. Her face is hot when she touches it, her thighs are hot. Dreaming consummation, she achieved it.

Who was her lover?

At first she feels no shame, only a kind of wonder at the creative prowess of her brain-in-sleep. Imagination courted and readied her, imagination took her, and her body is glad to have been taken, if only in dreams.

Who was he?

Beyond the scrim of consciousness, she searches for his face, but it remains hidden from her in mist and shadow. She remembers his touch, the electric clarity of hands gentle and intelligent on her body, the moist of his breath on cheek and belly.

But who?

Her dreams are seldom so hard to recall. It is as if, with this evasion, one part of her mind wishes to spare another pain, but she insists on knowing.

WHO.

She seizes the image of a hand and holds it fast, with dream eyes proceeds from shapely wrist to elbow, from biceps to slope of shoulder to curve of neck, from neck to jaw.

She lifts her eyes and knows, and knowledge strikes her with the force of a blow. Alice leans back into her rumpled pillows and pushes her damp hair back off her forehead. She stares into the darkness as it were her self. And knows.

It was Bartholomew.

13

INTO THE DARKNESS music comes, at first, the solitary trill of a flute, soon joined by muted wood-on-wood percussion. A blue light rises on the convex screen, and as it does, etches in silhouette the score or so of bodies that intervene between her and it. They still stir, settling in; their shoulders lift or twist or shift a little, side to side. Near the front, someone coughs. A black crow, crossing the screen in an arc, defines the blue as sky. Even as the image is absorbed and the identification accepted, accompanied by a surge of violins, the blue begins to change, to deepen until it is no longer entirely blue but blue/green, pure color put in motion by the shifting of light in its depths. A naked woman torpedoes through the water, spinning as she swims, and Alice hears the involuntary exclamations of the audience as they once again grasp a temporarily withheld reality. Most of her colleagues still can't look at the People without pity or revulsion.

Another swimmer, male, with a large pointed head and thin-limbed body, appears on the screen, swimming parallel to the first but in the opposite direction. Both leave the frame, filled only, for the moment, with the water and the shifting light that makes its subtle currents visible, before they approach and pass again, their directions this time reversed.

The camera follows the spiral-swimming female as she arches up out of the water, then dives below its surface, her body near pool-bottom striped with light. She rises from the dive, and as her body reaches the surface and breaks it, becomes through some magic a water bird, taking flight from the ruffled surface of a gray/blue pond. The sound track rises with her and woman becomes bird, achieving wholeness in bird form. She flies. She flies away, and then is there again in the glowing water, now with her partner swimming patterns among four limbless bodies, torsos with neither arms nor legs, that float serenely and describe, collectively, the square of the dance.

The music softens and a woman's voice, clear and precise, speaks above it: "The music tells me how the dance should be. I hear quiet places in the music, I hear the little silences, and this gives me the idea to put the limbless ones in the dance."

The Fathers watch intently.

14

THE COCKTAIL HOUR has a feeling of reunion to it. Convocations of the Team are widely enough spaced in time that the process of maturation, or decline, is clearly evident. Hair is lost or lightened, marital status and professional affiliation change, one is fatter or thinner than last time. Now Thomas Allworthy—who must have been Alice's age now when she first met him—is dead, and they all feel his absence, less as loss, it seems to her, than as a measure of the passing years. More than once, she's been called upon to lift her margarita glass to drink his memory, more than once reminded in doing so how mortality encroaches on them all. The new man, dark haired and slim-hipped, whom she takes for Allworthy's successor, moves easily and is attractive.

The military barmen, dressed in epauletted white, look more prepossessing than the vacation-motley scientists and social scientists they serve. Pat Erwin makes his fourth trip to the bar. Either she's shrunk with age, or Larry Dixon has taken to wearing elevator shoes. Dr. Allingham hasn't changed her hairstyle, a neat French roll, in sixteen years. Several of the men have been Alice's lovers in the past, alumni of short-lived liaisons. Only Herb Stoller ever tried to extend an affair beyond the duration of a convention, only he ever visited her at the Place or slept in her bed there. Age works on him a process of diminution; still trim, he seems less robust, his skin thinner than it used to be. Now, in middle age, he wears his glasses all the time. As they talk, she searches for and finds the tiny lens-bisecting line that means bifocals.

"What interested me most, Alice, was the metaphoric equation of bird and swimmer in that tape. What role did language play in that, do you think?"

Herb is a linguist, the language Father. Alice remembers that he always talked throughout their lovemaking, as if his body needed words to instruct his pleasure. "Very little role, I think," she tells him. "The person who made the tape is highly visually oriented."

"What sex?" Herb asks. His current obsession is, she knows, the sexual biases of language.

"Both. Bartholomew's an hermaphrodite. He has fully developed organs of both sexes."

Herb whistles. "I wish I could recruit him for my experiments. He'd make the perfect control."

"Not unless you gave him a full deck of pronouns to play with," she says. Her eyes scan while Herb considers, and when they touch upon the new man, inadvertently meet his eyes. Her gaze reels him in; he wends his way among the drinkers and approaches smiling. So it begins. She feels a flutter of pulse in her carotid, the little chemical surge—estrogen or adrenaline? of her body making ready for flirtation.

He extends his hand to her. "I'm Jerome Kleig. And you're Mother Teresa of the Mutants. I've been eager to meet you, Dr. Halliburton."

"Really?"

Kleig smiles, a smile haloed in dark beard. "I expected someone older and less charming."

Adrenaline. His formidable confidence makes her combative. "I'm forty-two years old," she says, "and not particularly charming."

"I'm curious," Kleig says. "Tell me why you volunteered."

"I was recruited."

"No tragic love affair?"

"I'm a trained anthropologist."

Kleig nods. "With an undergraduate major in drama. Anthropology's gain is Broadway's loss."

"At the Place," Alice tells him, "there is no flattery. Our language is nonmanipulative."

"Your acting skills must serve you well."

"I'm quite comfortable in my role by now." Her role now is prim, professional; she senses that he likes to spar.

"And with your costume, scales and all?"

"Scales are a relatively common genetic mutation, Doctor, as you know. Somewhat less common than fur, more so than feathers. My scales are quite resplendent. I rather like them."

"Does every woman dream of being a goddess?"

"My tasks are primarily administrative," she says.

"Not the Great Mother?"

"Hardly. It seems you know more about me than about the Place. Our language recognizes neither sex nor status difference. Brother Alice has his work, just as everyone else does."

Instead of answering, he looks beyond her, and Alice wonders if she's been too convincingly aloof. He *is* attractive, and a good opponent. Perhaps it's time to show him that capitulation is not impossible. His dark eyes return to her, their intensity unsettling, and Alice realizes she has no very clear idea of what he intends, or what she wants to happen.

The maitre d' announces lunch. Kleig takes her empty glass and puts it on a passing waiter's tray, then offers his escort arm to her. "Shall we, Brother?"

With a deep breath, she accepts the offered arm, and Kleig guides them surely through the intervening confusion to the table of Project Director Harris Briggs, the father of the Fathers. Kleig's touch is both proprietary and full of promise. Alice is momentarily confused by the intricacy of the table setting, by the bewildering array of silver utensils that flanks her plate and the complexities of the half-forgotten social game they all must play. For a moment, she thinks with longing of the Place, then raises to her table-mates the very brightest of her unmasked smiles.

15

IT IS TIME, Harris Briggs informs the Team, to face up to new and frightening political realities.

The Team, arrayed in folding chairs before his podium, has no choice but to face Briggs or his realities. Alice sits to the rear of the conference room, near the door, Kleig near the front. His shoulders rise above the chair back, his head rises above other, surrounding heads, its tilt attentive. She sees the twin sworls of a double cowlick in his dark hair.

The economy continues to deteriorate, Briggs tells them. He summons a platoon, a regiment, a whole army of statistics to verify this assertion.

Alice tends to believe it—they say the same things often enough on television—though the whole question seems vaguely unreal to her. Her paycheck keeps coming in good times and bad, though she has no chance and little desire to spend it. She did notice, venturing into a department store to buy a dress before the conference, that it cost several times as much as the dress she bought for the conference five years ago, though the dresses differ substantially only in color. The new one is black. Attractive, she hopes. She hopes Kleig likes it.

"Gone," says Briggs, "are carte blanche budgets for social programs. The current Administration is intent on tightening the belts of the poor."

Again, he reiterates the nightly news. Alice is willing to be offended by such policies, but her outrage feels hollow. Abstraction militates against compassion. No one she knows is hungry, or unemployed. Her sister's husband just got a raise. She got a raise herself. Six rows in front of her, Kleig scratches his ear.

"Within government, competition for dwindling dollar resources is intense," Briggs says.

There is no money at the Place, and as a society, it functions as well as any she's seen or studied. Abolish money, she sometimes mutely advises the solons on her television screen, and half your problems will solve themselves. Simplistic, she knows. The Place has no resources, generates no product, is anything but self-supporting. She doesn't keep its books or pay its bills and when, come spring, she scans its budget is always staggered by the bottom line. Social perfection is stunningly expensive. If the People had to hunt or gather to survive, they'd all be dead.

"The budget of each federal agency is now subject to intense scrutiny," Briggs says. "The danger of discovery increases daily."

The Place is a secret kept from bureaucrats, from intelligence agencies, from accountants. Congress knows nothing of it. No President since John Kennedy chartered it has heard of its existence. Even the Pentagon is ignorant of it. They use a military conference center now disguised as a special study group reporting to the Nuclear Regulatory Commission, of which Harris Briggs, a nuclear physicist, is senior member. The project is a thief in the night, an invisible parasite sucking what blood it needs in small doses. Its funding sources are diffused throughout the individual budgets of no less than nineteen federal agencies, coded as the least conspicuous of line items: Additional Office Supplies; Supplementary Research and Development; Employee Recreation; Equipment Contingency; Bottled Water; Other. Each agency is billed regularly, if inauthentically. Each pays promptly. Bartholomew and

Kleig fuse in her mind. A free-floating desire envelopes her—a warmth, and the conviction that something is going to happen.

"If *this* President were to learn of our existence," Briggs says, "there's no certainty that he would sympathize with the objectives of our charter, or even permit the project to survive."

The charter of the Place is, of course, a high-sounding humanitarian document. The political realities that spawned it were somewhat less sublime. As early as 1961, Kennedy's Brain Trust began to warn of coming energy shortages so severe they might trigger profound economic and social instability, even revolution. The answer, they counseled, was locked in the atom. Unleash it and be free. At the same time, an alarming number of genetic abnormalities, suspected to be phenotypic expressions of genetic damage, were occurring among the offspring of nuclear plant workers regularly exposed to radiation. Reports of burgeoning mutations so alarmed the President that he was ready to stop the atom-splitters entirely.

His concern was misplaced, his advisors told him, his priorities were out of scale. Compared to the fate of the free world, suspended in the balance, the human cost was really, relatively speaking, almost negligible. Atomic energy development *must* proceed, preferably without a lot of bad press about babies born blind or legless. The champions of development hatched a plan: the government could build a refuge for these unfortunate genetic misfits, these victims of inevitable progress; they could be well cared for, and their parents need never suffer knowing they survived. Tell them their children were born dead. It was only later, when the children of too many nuclear plant workers were born dead, that the project hit upon the scheme of substituting healthy babies for the damaged ones.

The President bought it. It seemed to give him the chance to do right both politically and morally. Other of his advisors embellished the idea until it seemed irreproachably humane. The refuge would be no mere holding pen, no human dump, but a carefully planned, self-contained community conceived and engineered by the best minds in America. Its residents would receive excellent medical care and abundant aesthetic experience. No unscrupulous scientist would ever be allowed to experiment with their bodies or their minds. They would live out their lives with dignity. America owed them that much. If this selfless expression of American idealism happened to solve a nagging public relations problem, too, so much the better. Virtue is *supposed* to be its own reward.

Often, Alice has wondered which weighed heavier—conscience or expedience. But John Kennedy is long dead, the Place lives on, and time, with its inevitable statute of limitations, has made the question of motivations irrelevant. Her own motivations are beyond analysis. Too simple. Too complex.

Somewhere in the left front quadrant of the room, a hand shoots up, interrupting Briggs's doomish monologue and Alice's internal one. Briggs glares at the owner of the hand; she cranes to see whose hand it is.

"Dr. Singh?"

Singh's English is truly cosmopolitan; it smacks equally of Oxford and Bombay. He is unfailingly, almost archaically polite. Politely, he inquires if it might not be possible to take a small break before continuing. His request is timely. Expecting acquiescence, the members of the Team sit straighter, the shuffling of their papers makes an end-of-meeting noise, but Briggs, behind his podium, refuses to dismiss them. "I am almost done with my remarks. I would prefer to continue." His audience settles back, recrossing legs, supining lower spines, resigned.

"With more plants on line, and more of these approaching obsolescence, our clientele is greater than ever before. The step-up in plutonium production contributes, as does the elevated birth rate. Suddenly it seems it's fashionable among the baby-boomers to have babies. Target children are being born at the rate of five to twelve per month. In fact, the time to consider establishing a second facility approaches fast."

Next to Alice, Dr. Fisher whispers to Dr. Weiss. "We could start a franchise operation, like McDonald's. Charge per capita, per annum." Dr. Weiss snickers. Dr. Briggs silences them with an arctic look. Alice tries to imagine a second Place, a third and fourth, a chain of Places, an endless succession of silver-scaled administrators, herself compounded endlessly. Her desire exponentially increased.

"We all agree, I believe, that our project serves a vital function. None of us, I'm sure, wishes to see our work curtailed. But in order to continue, possibly to expand in times like these, we must be willing to consider radical alternatives."

I am, Alice thinks. I do. Bartholomew is a radical alternative to a most ancient problem. Whom shall I love?

Briggs drops his eyes to his watch face, then raises them to Singh. "There, Doctor, I'm done. Soon enough, I trust. Tomorrow we'll resume our discussion of what those alternatives might be. Please note that this evening, Dr. Allingham will present a paper entitled 'The Reduction of Societal Stress Through Diet Management' in Salon B. In Salon C, doctors Tyler and Weiss will debate the question 'Does Loss of Ritual Passage Mechanisms Contribute to Delinquency Among Adolescent Males?' The squash courts and saunas will be open until ten P.M. Cocktail hour is six to seven." The black dress, surely. A radical alternative to silver scales.

Briggs steps down from his patriarchal platform and a number of his colleagues, Kleig among them, throng to applaud or comment on his speech. Briggs was astute, she thinks, more so than usual, to stop when and where he did, to formulate the question without answering it. Alice turns it in her mind: What is the quid pro quo?

16

FOR A MOMENT, the waning crescent moon appears to be the squint-eye of an angry dragon, scouring the darkened earth for prey, and Bartholomew fears for the Place. Then, as he watches, a wind from the south attenuates the clouds, tapering the head of the beast into a dove's head, its crescent eye benign. Seconds later, the dove's eye becomes the bill of a duck, upcurved, and then the moon is gone entirely behind a thickening gauze of clouds. The cold penetrates his clothing and shrinks his skin; soon it will snow. In darkness, he rolls on. The dragon in the sky, ephemeral, lives on in his mind.

It is too early yet for the messengers, or for Brother Alice's call, his vigil is useless, yet it pleases him to keep it. Sleep would be impractical. None of the People is awake to bear him company. There is nothing to do but wait, and his waiting feels both ritual and proper, as though it proves his loyalty or fills some unexplained but pressing need. In the office, he stares a long while at Brother Alice's portrait, aligning memory to recorded image and missing him. Tonight the beast looked and passed on without striking, tonight the People are safe, but his sense of danger is not so easily dispelled.

When the black-cloaked messengers have come and gone, William jocular and friendly, Fritz taciturn, Bartholomew turns off the office lights to wait beside the phone. The eyes of the Fathers, he sometimes thinks, look at him from the wall clock's face, all-knowing and reproachful; in the dark, he and the clock are invisible to one another, though he can still hear it spitting out minutes, one by one, deliberately.

There is deliberate gaiety in Brother Alice's voice. "Has the Place survived another day without me?"

Bartholomew's yes is solemn. "I hope so."

"You're not sure?"

Bartholomew says nothing of the dragon in the sky. "One of the youngsters came today to ask me about the Excitement. He was afraid he was sick."

Brother Alice laughs. "What did you tell him?"

"I told him not to be afraid. That it's natural for our bodies to feel pleasure, and that his does means that he'll come of age soon. Then he asked me why it happens."

"What did you say?"

"I said it was one of the mysteries."

"Was he satisfied?"

"I'm not sure," Bartholomew says. "I'm not sure that I am."

The long silence on the phone line convinces him he was wrong to say so, but when Brother Alice speaks, it is only to say, "Oh?" The voice does not condemn, and the faint rise of a question encourages him to go on. "Sometimes," Bartholomew says, "I think the mysteries are doors we could unlock if we had the right keys. Sometimes I want to know what lies behind them."

"What lies behind them," Brother Alice says, "is more locked doors. Always more. Even the Fathers can't open all of them."

Bartholomew's surprise is genuine. "They can't?"

"No, they can't. And sometimes they open doors they shouldn't. They open the wrong door and let the beast escape."

Bartholomew thinks of the clouds. "What beast?" he asks. "What does it look like?"

Brother Alice says, "Not a real one, Bartholomew. It's just a figure of speech. Saying one thing to mean another. What I mean is, knowledge can be dangerous as well as good."

"Because it makes you want more knowledge?" he asks, but when Brother Alice speaks again, his voice is distant, precisely as if a door, once open, had closed between them. "Don't worry about it, Bartholomew. It's not your problem. Just keep things running until I get back."

"I'll try," he promises. "When will you get back?"

"Soon, I hope." Then another door closes. "Good night, Bartholomew."

Alice drops the receiver into its cradle beside the bed. Just in time. Every time she talks to Bartholomew, she says too much, she puts his innocence at peril. Something in her, not quite pure, seems tempted constantly to spoil his purity. She gets out of bed, her cotton nightgown light against her body, feet bare in the carpet's deep pile. Behind the thick stiff draperies, she half expects to find blank wall, but there is glass, fogged by the clash of temperatures, the modulated cool inside meeting, on its surface, the desert night. It's true: she would give him the world, the whole great universe, known and conjectured, and say to him, "There now, what can you make of that?"

A longing fills her, so big and deep she is surprised her body can contain it. She wipes a patch of moisture from the window glass, and then sees clearly how the sentinel saguaros, stretching uneven arms, reach to hold up an earthward crescent moon.

17

THE MORNING SESSION CONVENES. Alice tries to focus her sleep-starved brain. Radical alternatives, that's it. Most of the Team appears attentive, as if they'd rested well. Alice is surprised but not displeased when Briggs begins by introducing their new colleague, Dr. Jerome Kleig of Stanford, derives what personal history she can from his credential acronyms as Briggs recites them. Kleig disappeared soon after last night's dinner; the flirtation did not progress, though she persists in believing that it will. Last night, she declined to visit the sauna with her old friend Herb Stoller, though it would have been a harmless entertainment. As Kleig mounts the platform, his step is spritely. There's no denying the fact he's younger by some than she is.

He begins by scanning the audience, and she feels the brief touch of his gaze. Her nervous system responds with a low buzz audible only to herself that deafens her temporarily to what Kleig says. When it subsides, she joins his speech in progress.

"We believe, Dr. Briggs and I, that the climate in Washington today promises doom unless we act boldly to counteract it. The humanitarian foundation on which this project rests is not, and we must face it, strong enough to withstand the storm tides of fiscal reform.

"Consider. Our President and his point men have already displayed their willingness to reduce environmental protections, to open federal lands to commercial exploitation, and to try to stimulate the economy by raising military spending to wartime levels. It has long been felt within the project that our trump card is the threat of public disclosure, yet I believe that while this would have deterred former Presidents from scuttling our work, this Administration is perfectly capable of viewing such a threat as nothing more serious than another public relations challenge.

"Imagine it. The President at his Oval Office desk, his speech on cue cards, a photograph of the first lady beaming out at the TV audience. He has a chart behind him. He points to it. It shows how relatively small the entire mutant population is in comparison to the numbers of healthy Americans gainfully employed in the interlocking civilian and military nuclear power industries. He smiles. He chuckles. America believes he's a nice guy. They buy it.

"And zam—your people are mainstreamed or worse yet, thrown on corporate charity. Not a nice scenario, but an increasingly plausible one, I'm afraid. What can we do to stop it?"

Clotho on welfare, Boris on the assembly line. And on the midway, Bartholomew, the Dolphin Boy/Girl. Two freaks in one. The world Kleig evokes is pitiless. She does not want to believe in its reality. WHAT CAN WE DO?

"Simply put, we have to offer a return on the investment made in us, and fortunately, this should be relatively easy to do."

He unhands the podium and leans back slightly. "As we all know, this Administration, more than any other, is willing to contemplate nuclear military engagement. We have a President who is willing, perhaps even eager, to press the button. He practices brinksmanship, but there is every indication that he is, if provoked, quite willing to cross the brink.

"He needs information, of the kind we are uniquely positioned to provide. How will the human species sur-

vive on a contaminated earth, on severely limited resources? What does the future hold for the race? In-
deed, does the race have a future? These questions
loom large. And we can answer many of them.

"Our clients *are* the second generation. From autop-
sies and tissue samples, we've learned a good deal about
the chromosomal effects of radiation exposure, but several pressing questions remain unanswered. Clearly,
the greatest of these concerns the reproductive viabil-
ity of this second generation. Can they reproduce
themselves, and with what result?"

This is not the answer she expected. This is not the
answer. Her desire turns to shame, something dead and
putrifying trapped inside her. As a nightmare perse-
veres, so does Kleig.

"I know you consider this train of thought anathema,
many of you," Kleig goes on. "I know the language and
the culture of the Place have been deliberately con-
structed to prevent mating, even to prevent the population from knowing that such a thing as sex exists.
Perhaps this was a kindness, perhaps not. But in her
reports, Dr. Halliburton, who knows the population
better than anyone, muses that some mutations may be
compensatory or absolutely beneficial. She goes so far
as to speculate that certain of what we consider handi-
caps may actually represent evolutionary shortcuts to
desirable ends."

A number of her colleagues turn their heads in search
of her; their gazes, settling, seem to accuse. Alice's face
burns. Her monthly reports have gone unread so long
that over the years she's come almost to regard them as
a personal journal, or a piece of speculative literature
composed for an ideal other—herself without the par-
ticularity of her experience. She half rises, intending to
say, "Dr. Kleig misinterprets my position," something

to acquit her from charges of collusion, but Harris Briggs himself waves her down. "There will be ample time for discussion after Dr. Kleig has finished his presentation."

"If we were to undertake a controlled breeding program within the population," Kleig says, "we could learn in a matter of a few years what would otherwise require decades. I believe it's not possible to overestimate the value of this information to our political leaders. The financial future of our project would be assured."

Kleig smiles. "Many other experiments, too, could yield valuable knowledge. Since our data collection methods have been indirect, we've had no opportunity to study the whole living organism, or its response to environmental pressures. Scores of anatomical, physiological and psychological questions remain to be answered. We can answer them, and those answers will contribute profoundly to our understanding of the species, present and potential. With so much good to be achieved, I see no reason not to commence at once."

Silence greets his enthusiasm, and Alice finds it a hard silence to read. The quiet she contributes is speechless outrage, a sense of violation.

Kleig says, "And, of course, our studies could be made public. Our findings could be published and shared."

In the rows before her, Alice sees a few backs straighten. It's been a dilemma for many of the Team, that because of the secrecy of its subject, much of their best work has gone unpublished and uncelebrated. That her colleagues were willing to accept this professional liability, Alice has always taken as proof of their worth. There have been jokes, too, of course—mock threats to publish, a proposal to claim access to an extraterrestrial population, another to establish a Nobel

Prize for distinguished work in classified areas—but no one, to her knowledge, has ever violated his vow of public silence.

"I've worked extensively to devise a controlled breeding program that would yield maximum data in the shortest possible time," Kleig says. "I would be delighted to hear from you or work with you to develop other experiments that promise to prove equally efficient and provocative."

Kleig's sincerity appears unquestionable. Within the outline of his beard, his cheeks wear the flush of conviction, his eyes are not the eyes of a malefactor. Perhaps it's only devil's advocacy he practices. She waits for Harris Briggs to tell them it's all a joke, an elaborate ruse meant to challenge their integrity, or strengthen their collective resolve. Please give the punch line that will deliver us from evil.

None comes, and no one else seems to expect it. Around her, her colleagues are thoughtful, grave, but not outraged. They seem able to accept this inversion of reality with equanimity. Their faces appear freakishly the same to her, their symmetry the endless and unprofitable repetition of a worn idea. Alice is not of them, will not be of them. She lets her mind fly home, she lets her thoughts flee to the Place.

"I'll entertain your questions now," says Harris Briggs.

18

Barmew, Barmew
He chews his milk, he drinks his meat
He has two wheels instead of feet
Listen when he speaks to you
Barmew, Barmew.

THE SMALL ONES dance around his chair, singing their new song. Joseph made it up. Some of the children worried that Bartholomew would be offended by the part about his having no feet, but when they asked him, he told them no, he didn't mind because it was true. He joins in the singing, and they repeat the one verse again and again until the song dissolves in breathless laughter. In his bed, watching, Joseph wears an instigator's smile.

Tired from their game, the children sprawl on the floor around Bartholomew and demand that he tell them a story.

"Once there was a duck," he begins, "a young duck who lived on the pond in the gardens. He was a brown duck with a white collar and a green head, and his name was Joseph. At first, Joseph was afraid of people, and ran to hide when they came to the gardens. But one small person came every day to sit by the pond, and little by little, Joseph got used to seeing him there, and little by little, he got less afraid. One day when he came to sit beside the pond, the small one looked so sad that Joseph decided he would try to cheer him up. Slowly, he waddled out of his hiding place under a big bush and went to the small one.

" 'What's wrong?' he asked in duck talk. 'Why are you sad?' "

Brutus appears in the doorway, tall in his white nurse's smock. "Bartholomew, Dorian just called on the intercom. They want you at the poolhouse."

Bartholomew stops talking duck talk. "Did he say why?"

Brutus shakes his head. "He didn't say. But they want you to come quickly."

The small ones groan. *Don't go, Barmew. Stay and finish our story.* The boldest children clutch the arms of his chair.

"I have to go," he says. "But Joseph will finish the story. I know he can."

"But I don't know the end of the story, Barmew," Joseph protests.

Bartholomew laughs, extricating himself from the gaggle of small ones. "Neither do I," he says. "You'll have to make it up."

It's moistly warm in the poolhouse, and the air, like the water, has a blue/green chlorine tang. No music plays, and several of the People stand beside the pool, staring fixedly into the water. Bartholomew joins them. In the water, a body floats facedown, a slim brown body with one arm, one leg. Leda.

"What happened?" Bartholomew asks.

The poolkeeper, Dorian, answers. "He was swimming. I watched for a while, then went to fold the towels. When the others came to swim, they found him. We called his name. He won't answer. He doesn't move."

Two of the People are naked for swimming, and Bartholomew asks them to get into the pool. They maneuver Leda's body to the edge and slide the straps of the derrick under it. Rising, it hangs heavy. A wheelchair waits at poolside, and they try to settle Leda in it but his body is stiff and won't conform to the shape of the chair.

He stares at Bartholomew without recognition, and his face wears the expression Bartholomew has often seen there, mouth open to draw a swimmer's breath, his features all involved in the task, the whole look, normally fleeting, of an exhilaration beyond mere pleasure. It persists horribly. Bartholomew closes Leda's eyelids. His flesh feels like wet rubber. They all know, but none will say it. It falls to Bartholomew to give death a name.

"Leda has gone to the Fathers," he says. "He died doing what he loved best, without suffering. We'll miss him."

Dorian approaches Bartholomew, his pink eyes wavering with tears. "I'd like to play Leda's music," he says. "Maybe it will speed him on his way."

Bartholomew agrees and Dorian shuffles off. Seconds later, the poolhouse is full of music, of violins and lyrical percussion, the same music that scores the tape of Leda and the birds. Bartholomew remembers editing the tape, playing over and over again each movement of the dance until it became indelible in his brain, inseparable from himself, until with his eyes closed, he could feel the currents of the water warm and sleek against his body, until he could spin like a bullet through the water, until he could swim with Leda in the pool and share the exaltation that lit his face. Part of him will always swim with Leda, and he is not ashamed of the tears that fall freely from his eyes.

The two swimmers dive into the pool and swim hard, lap after lap. Dorian, who knew Leda so well, sits beside his body, holding the lifeless hand. At last, Bartholomew wipes away his tears and says, "I have to call the nurses now. Leda's body must go to the doctors."

Dorian nods, and Bartholomew feels in his resignation a sort of gratitude; he doesn't want to be responsible. Distantly, the dinner bell rings. The swimmers climb out of the pool and go to dress. Dorian still clings to Leda's hand. "Go eat," Bartholomew tells him. "You need to be with the People. I'll wait for the nurses."

Dorian gives Leda's hand a final pat and lets it fall. Before he leaves, he lets his hand rest for a moment on Leda's short curly hair. "Already dry," he says, and shakes his head.

Bartholomew does not know how to be alone with the dead, whether he should look at the body or try to ignore it. Does anything of his friend remain? He whispers Leda's name and scans the whole corpse, face and body, for some sign of response. None comes. The symphony ends and leaves the poolhouse quiet. Bartholomew's own breathing sounds very loud. A sense of incompletion nags him, but he can think of nothing more to do. Bartholomew hopes that for Leda death is flying, that he will learn to swim through air. He doesn't know if what he feels is grief, or simple loneliness, or if they are the same.

There are hours still to wait for Brother Alice's call.

19

"I PRESCRIBE REST AND RECREATION, Dr. Halliburton. Have dinner with me tonight," he said.

"I don't think so," she said.

"You spend too much of your life in compounds," he said. "There's a place nearby where we can eat and drink and even dance."

"I haven't danced since 1965," she said. "Besides, haven't you heard? We're not allowed to leave the premises until the conference is over."

"I have a special dispensation. Or are you afraid to be alone with me?"

"I'm not afraid of anything. But if you think you can win me over to your side, you're wrong. Don't even try."

"It wasn't my intention to lobby you, Doctor. At least not entirely. Consider this. You might enjoy yourself."

"I might not."

"Would you like it better if I said I wanted to learn more about your work?"

"Not after the way you distorted what you read in my reports."

"I'll pick you up at seven," Kleig said. "Wear something pretty."

How she dislikes him for saying that, three words so full of presumptions. As if she should find it necessary to please him. As if she should want to. Worse yet, as if what they are engaged in is some kind of mating dance, requiring a ritual display of plumage. Her civilian wardrobe is small and utilitarian, composed of one uniform tailored for each kind of occasion she is likely to encounter in the outside world. She wishes she could wear her silver scales and metal arm, that she could turn her wise green higher eye on Kleig. Brother Alice is powerful, and no matter how powerful the emotions that rise up inside the silver suit, he

she

The search for a pronoun stops her.

It almost stops her heart.

She freezes in front of the bathroom mirror, a mirror crowned by a row of light bulbs to promote a fantasy of stardom, so long that the soap on her face begins to dry, makes her skin feel taut, then almost solid, threatens to make her look of confusion, this slit-mouthed blank, a permanent expression. Only her eyes seem alive in the white mask, and she finds no certainty in them, no reassurance, but only a sort of desperation. Her pupils are dilated widely, the irises two thin blue rims encircling blackness. The aperture both draws and frightens her, as though, if she looked too long into her mirrored eyes, she might be totally absorbed, she might be sucked up into the image, be turned inside out and cease to exist objectively, on this side of the mirror.

There is a powerful sense of invitation—let go, let go —and an equally powerful fear of letting go. If she looks into her eyes, which are not wholly or simply her own, something big and irremediable will happen to her, she will see or feel or understand something absolute, over which she will have no control. She will never have control again. One small part of her remains a coach on the sidelines of the struggle, a rational voice exhorting her to face it down. The world is predictable and three-dimensional and dull. Nothing will happen. Nothing can. The only danger is cowardice. And yet she knows she is in peril.

Water rushing from the spigot fills the closed basin, it overflows, and the splash of cold water on her stomach, running down her thighs, breaks the trance. Automatically she turns the faucet off, unplugs the bowl and watches the water whirlpool quickly down the drain, away. She's made a mess. Water shines the yellow tile and she stands in a puddle. Fortunately the army is generous with towels; the maids leave more, plush and absorbent, each day than she could use in a week. She throws several on the floor to blot up the flood.

Twenty minutes lost. She turns efficient, scrubbing off the soap, smoothing lotion on her skin. Her eyes in the mirror are exceedingly bright. What set her off? She searches her memory until she finds the trigger, and the strength of the revelation, its simplicity, makes her laugh out loud. Of course.

Of course she's confused. It's only natural, an occupational hazard of her singular profession. Of course she's drawn to Bartholomew; they have ambivalence in common.

Or maybe it's not either/or, she thinks, but both, a strength. Perhaps we *are* the blessed.

She laughs again, painting her cheeks pink and her lips red, brushing her short dark woman hair until it crackles. She zips a blue dress, plain but sleek, onto her woman body, slides her stockinged feet into the most improbable of woman shoes, shiny black and insubstantial, and feels as if she has just remembered something she has always known and only temporarily forgotten. A slight, straight woman turns a slow pirouette before her bedroom mirror and knows that in some measure, imperceptible but absolutely real, beyond petty conventions of dress, of language or preference in mating, she is a man, as well.

When Kleig arrives, a few minutes after the hour, she is ready for him, receptive to his admiration, unafraid. His Porsche seems predictable, somehow. Strapped into the supple leather seat, Alice plays passenger to his pilot. Kleig's hand rests always on the gearshift, his eyes scan the gauges and dials on the dashboard, and any conversation he carries on is with the engine, which speaks to him in a throaty monotone, accented with a roar when he shifts gears. He pushes her into fourth quickly. Alice watches the speedometer needle drift steadily upward until it reaches and comes to rest at 95. "I love these desert roads," Kleig says. "Best gas mileage you'll ever get."

She smiles. The highway is straight and flat and empty, a swath cut through the desert scruff. A luminous twilight engulfs them. The glowing green outline of a cocktail glass, stirred crudely by a pixilated swizzle stick, appears like a mirage on the horizon, just to the right of the vanishing point, and grows as they approach it until Alice can see the neon olive drowning in its depths.

Inside, the roadhouse has a western motif—the walls hung with antique guns and the heads of dead animals. The glass eyes of a moose, a buffalo, a wolf stare balefully down upon the diners. There are others, too, large and small, horned or hairy, that she can't name by species. The waitresses wear abbreviated buckskin skirts and vests and carry their order pads in holsters on their hip-slung belts. She sees neither a jukebox nor a band, but the place is filled with a whiny instrumental lament that distracts her at first but soon recedes into a kind of purple noise meant, she guesses, to soothe and isolate the clientele. A waitress comes, fringe twitching pertly, to ask if they would like a drink.

Alice orders scotch. She always orders scotch. She has one stock drink, just as she has one stock dress, one pair of earrings for wearing in the outside world. Kleig asks for a martini, dry. "What are you thinking?" he asks.

To answer truthfully, *I no longer understand the context we occupy* seems both too honest and too rude. She reverts to an earlier thought: "I was wondering if the rest of the buffalo is still intact on the other side of the wall."

"Not the most tasteful decor, I'll admit," Kleig says. "But more amusing than the barracks, don't you think? I have the ubiquitous Monet seascapes in my room."

"I have Degas," she tells him. "Fat dancers bathing after a hard rehearsal. I can't help wondering what the visiting generals make of them."

"I never dated a nun before," Kleig says, dismissing the Impressionists.

Alice loses the chance to say she suspects Degas of misogyny. "You seem to think there's something world-renouncing about my work," she says instead.

"There's not?"

"I don't think so. No."

"Explain yourself." He serves the words up with a smile, but his tone is commanding, and she accepts the challenge. Brother Alice is never called to account, Dr. Alice only rarely. "I always wanted to do field work, but by the time I came along, all those wonderful little pockets of primitive culture had already been turned inside out. The Place is probably as close as one can come in the world today to a wholly isolated society." She pauses to sip from her scotch. "Put it this way. I doubt Margaret Mead would have turned the job down, either."

"Margaret Mead's been married—how many times?"

"I understand she practices serial monogamy, yes."

"You've been at the Place for sixteen years."

Alice smiles. "The money's very good."

"I don't believe you do it for the money."

"You're right. I have no use for money."

Kleig puts his forearms on the table and leans toward her. "You're an attractive woman, Alice."

She pauses briefly to savor the compliment, no matter how mendacious, before rebuffing it. "Fortunately, that's not considered a disqualification for meaningful work."

"Is your work meaningful?" he asks.

"God yes. Isn't yours?"

Evidently he didn't expect a question; he explores his moustache with an index finger, delicately, as though he hoped to find an answer among the bristles. She presses her point. "Well?"

"Well," Kleig says. "The data I collect is mostly self-referential. It can take hundreds of little pieces puzzled together to explain one incredibly minute phenomenon. Even that may not have much meaning in your sense of the word."

"Which is?"

"Macroscopic. Humanistic. Probably, god help us, moralistic."

"Moral," she says. "And nonmanipulative."

Kleig laughs at her primness. "I prefer to think of it as intervention. Sometimes it becomes necessary to intervene."

"Are you a student of Machiavelli, Dr. Kleig?" Alice asks, but his reply is forestalled by the cowgirl waitress, bringing their meal. There is too much food on Alice's plate, more than she wants or needs. The excess embarrasses her. Kleig begins to partition his steak, bloodily rare, into bite-size cubes while she dresses her potato.

"What I wonder most is," Kleig says, "what do you do for sex?"

Alice is just able to meet his eyes, both brown. Her voice is Brother Alice's when she answers, "I'm not immune from the Excitement, Dr. Kleig."

He holds her gaze. "My name is Jerry, Alice, and I find it hard to believe you haven't had a lover in sixteen years."

Alice shrugs, wondering if the sex life he imagines for her is more or less exotic than the truth. In truth, she's tried most of the available solutions to the problem. One of them is to not think about sex until her dreams demand it.

"Well?" he asks.

"Tell me, Dr. Kleig, are you willing to share the intimate details of your personal life with me, or is this supposed to be a unilateral confession?"

"It's a practical question," he answers smoothly. "One I'd ask a prison inmate or an Arctic explorer. I know how you're fed and sheltered. I wonder how you satisfy your other basic human drives."

"How do you satisfy *your* basic human drives?" she asks. "I thought the procedure was pretty universal. If you're in doubt, though, I understand there are some good books on the subject."

"Logistics," Kleig says. "Procurement. I take it for granted you don't seduce the mutants."

She laughs. "Don't think I haven't been tempted, Kleig."

He assumes she's joking and laughs too.

"Actually, my rooms adjoin my office. None of the People has ever seen them. I do have privacy."

"And company?"

"I've had visitors from time to time."

"Male visitors, I presume."

"You are presumptuous," she says. "I've noticed that. And tell me about yourself, Jerry. Are you married?"

"I was married."

"To a woman?"

"Of course."

"What happened?" she asks, but he's reprieved from answering by the arrival of the band, four J.C. Penney cowboys in white Stetsons; keyboard, guitar, banjo and fiddle. A harmonica hangs from the neck of the fattest cowboy. From their costumes, she expects a hoedown, but when they play, it's country pop in ballad time. A couple rises to dance. Hugging each other tightly, they execute a spritely shuffle. Others, emboldened, join them. Kleig rises before asking, "Shall we?"

"I'm out of practice," she says on the way to the small dance floor. Kleig holds her hand. "I'm not," he says.

They embrace. He's taller than she, but not so much so that she can't see, over his shoulder, the self-induced sorrow on the singer's face as he mouths complaints about the injustices of love. The other couples swirl around them. Kleig drives her almost as skillfully as he does his sports car, signaling changes with a beat-long pause and new directions with a subtle pressure of his hand above her waist. The feel of him is compact; her hand on his back finds him lean, almost bony. When the song ends, he keeps his hand around her waist as the other men, husbands or lovers, do.

They dance again, and the music is faster, the rhythms more complex. He seems to identify with the fiddle, to emulate its melody with his movements. She would have chosen the keyboard, with its more emphatic beat, but he leads well and she follows him. As they dance, his thigh makes casual incursions against her thighs, her torso feels his torso through the layers of their clothing, warmth and shape and clash of fabrics. His right hand, chastely above her waist until now, moves down her back to the flat place just before her buttocks curve. She wants to do something equally proprietary to him, but what? To lay her cheek against his shoulder seems submissive, and there is no way for her to usurp the prerogative of leading. She has to content herself with lowering her left hand and letting her palm spread flat against his back.

When she does, he puts his second arm around her, closing the space between them. Her arm curls around his shoulders and their pelvises touch, each pair of their legs, his and hers, moves as one leg. Now and then she feels Kleig's genitals against her belly, the familiar warm bulge her high school partners used to tease her with as well, though Kleig is less reticent about it, more matter-of-fact than they. She finds that to call him Kleig in her mind, to mistrust him even as they reveal so much, so subtly, is exciting. She presses back, not lewdly, but enough to maintain contact, enough to let him know she does so. Sweat flowers on her face and the front of her body against his body, the places where his hands touch her back feel very warm. Alice thinks of Bartholomew. It would not be possible to dance this way with him.

They part after dancing, and she doesn't like the sudden coolness that envelopes her. Only their hands are joined. Kleig looks down at her, his smile surprisingly gentle. "You know I'm willing," he says.

She nods.

"Acknowledgment or agreement?"

"Both," she says, and holds herself tightly in her own arms on the short ride to the Sidewinder Motel, so that the necessary warmth won't dissipate. She waits in the

Porsche while he registers, and when he returns, asks him, "Who are we?"

"What? Oh. Mr. and Mrs. Jerry Hall. Part yours, part mine. We're also number ten."

Number ten is serviceable enough for trysting, air-conditioned and anonymous. Kleig experiments with the lighting until he finds what pleases him, the bathroom light left on, the door open, the bedroom illumined indirectly by escaping light.

"Would you like me to undress you, Brother Alice, or do you prefer to do it yourself?"

"Let me undress you first," she says, because she senses it will surprise him and because, having decided to allow herself the luxury of making love, she feels entitled to all constituent sensations.

"Stand there," she says, and begins with his tie, unbuttons his shirt to find his chest restates the theme of hair, dark and curly, clumped just above the hollow of his breastbone. She smiles when her hands come to the buckle of his belt and release it, sees he is embarrassed and amused at his own embarrassment and trying to enjoy it, too, as she unsnaps and unzips and eases the pinstriped blue pants down over his hipbones, then lets them fall into a pile around his ankles. Stands back a little to appreciate the package before she opens it, the sturdy white cotton Jockey shorts, and she imagines what's inside them; then, almost shyly, touches the white cotton bulge and feels its excitement and its warmth, and she wonders if she is really bold enough to put her fingers inside the waistband and pull down. Finally, slowly, she does, pulling the elastic away, away from his body and liking the sense of volition in his member as it springs free and stands erect, desire defying gravity as it stands out, straight, toward her.

He lets her look a moment, only a moment, before he

pulls her close and initiates a reciprocal disrobing. On the way to the bed, she hesitates, needing to state her terms. "This happens between equals, Doctor. No advantage to either side."

"Whatever you say, Doctor," Kleig agrees, then lifts her in his arms and lays her naked on cool coarse sheets. When she awakes suddenly, urgently, much later, the bathroom light still shines, Kleig sleeps, and her wristwatch says that it is well past three.

20

HE STOPS WAITING AT LAST, not because his waiting is fulfilled, but because his vigil has lost all object and all hope, because his capacity for waiting has been exhausted. Snow no longer falls, but has, while he waited, and his wheels hiss, laying tracks in the new white. It seems days, not hours, since Leda died and his grief feels frozen, as the surface of the pond is frozen, into something hard and motionless. The evergreens bordering the path are dusted white and a coat of ice shines on the bare limbs of the trees that lose their leaves. Knowing so little of the world beyond the Place, Bartholomew is unable to imagine excuses for Brother Alice's failure to call; first his body, now his voice have disappeared. Because he feels he should, Bartholomew keeps alive a dull, amorphous wish that no harm has befallen Brother Alice.

A light burns in the studio, but Ringer has fallen asleep waiting for him, his head turned sideways, resting on his arm. Though his body is still and without consciousness, Bartholomew knows instinctively that Ringer is alive, as surely as he knew that Leda was dead, and he wonders, watching him, what distinguishes the vacancy of sleep from the vacancy of death.

A touch recalls him; Ringer stirs, sighs, then raises his head. His pupils come to focus on Bartholomew. "Finally," he says. "I got tired, waiting for you."

"I was waiting, too. Now we've both stopped. What do you have to show me that won't keep till morning?"

"A tape," Ringer says.

"I never made a tape that wouldn't wait," Bartholomew tells him. "Or are you afraid it won't seem as good in the morning?"

Ringer stands, stretching his flesh limbs. "I didn't make this one. I found it."

"Is it mine?" Bartholomew asks.

Ringer shakes his head. "It came from the Fathers, in the last box of blanks. Somebody tried to erase it, but didn't quite succeed. The images are faint."

"What's on the tape? Is it the Fathers?"

"See for yourself." Ringer dims the lights and returns to the console. "I was getting ready to lay control track on the new tapes, not paying much attention, when I looked up at the monitor and there they were."

"Who?"

"I don't know who."

Ringer loads and starts the tape. Colored confetti, animated, fills the screen. The tape advances, but the signal doesn't change. "There's nothing," Bartholomew says.

"Wait."

They wait. Bartholomew is mesmerized by the dance of luminous particles on the face of the tube.

"Soon," Ringer says.

A figure appears, almost obscured by the blizzard of noise. A horizontal blip rides the up-scan, cycle after cycle, and the figure runs through static toward the camera, palsied by the blip. His face is ghostly through the noise but seems familiar, though Bartholomew is sure he's never seen him before. The next shot is from another camera in another place, a long shot that reveals a large, flattened circle around which many people run.

Now the camera moves close to one of the runners as he moves to the circumference and passes one, two, three of his fellows. Regular as a piston, his legs complete a circuit of rise, stretch, pound, his arms reach and retreat in alternation. The camera moves in, to show the taut cords of his muscles. On his face, Bartholomew recognizes the look of exhaustion and surpassing joy he sometimes saw on Leda's face. The runner thrusts out his chest and with it breaks through a ribbon stretched across his way. In slow motion the ribbon severs, its ends float in air. The runner slows his pace, then stops, bends almost double, gripping his ankles with his hands. The other runners catch him, slow, stop, bend as he did.

Ringer stops the tape, and they study the freeze frame. Form is apparent through the fog of interference. Bartholomew's eyes burn, his brain feels ponderously slow, yet he knows without being immediately able to say quite why that what he sees is devastatingly important. Ringer is sure to have theories, and he is sure to hear them. "Well?" he asks.

"There are people outside the Place," Ringer says. "People who are the same on both sides. They're stronger and wholer than our People."

"I wonder why they were running. What were they running from?"

"Don't be stupid, Bartholomew. It doesn't matter why they run. What matters is that they exist. The Fathers lied to us."

"We never asked them if there were other people who were the same on both sides," Bartholomew points out.

"We didn't know how, until now. They lied with their silence."

Bartholomew says, "I think our television is as good as theirs. Maybe better."

"They have three cameras. I counted. I can tell."

"Only two of us know how to use the cameras," Bartholomew says.

But Ringer won't be distracted, even by television. His eyes are bright, his fur bristles with curiosity and indignation, the set of his jaw is pugnacious. "What are we going to do?" he demands.

Bartholomew shrugs. "What I'm going to do is sleep. And then I'm going to think." He clings to the conviction that, with thinking, this new information can be explained, excused, made to fit with what he knows already, and believes. "You should, too," he counsels.

"I need to know," Ringer says, and Bartholomew sees it is his creed. Not knowing, to Ringer, is a form of torture. Sympathetic, he nods. "I know."

Questions pour out of Ringer with great velocity. Who are they? Why do they have three cameras? Why are they better than us? Why are we broken? Who broke us?

"I don't know," Bartholomew says.

"Brother Alice knows," Ringer says. "When is he coming back?"

"I don't know," Bartholomew says. His words both contain and conceal his doubt that Brother Alice is ever coming back. They are his answer to many questions now, about the world and his place in it. "I don't know," he says again. "I need to sleep."

21

DR. MASON SAYS TO DR. HALLIBURTON, "We missed you at dinner last night. I hope you weren't ill."

"Just tired," Dr. Halliburton says, the perfume of sex still lingering in her nostrils, beyond reach of the chemical euphemisms the others wear to disguise their natural human smells and not quite overridden by the scent of fear. "I spent a quiet evening."

To the Team, Harris Briggs says, "Let's talk this over." The colloquy begins. Its course, though it appalls her, does not surprise. Her science is one of observation; its authenticity depends upon the unobtrusiveness of the observer. Not so her colleagues'. Their disciplines require them to ask "What if?" They must create an empirical situation capable of answering their question. Their success derives from their manipulative ability, from the imagination and rigor of their interventions. Offered an expanded laboratory, they rush to take possession of it.

"There are at least four promising new cancer drugs that I'm aware of," Dr. Miller reports, "not yet tested on human subjects. The high incidence of cancer among the People would make the Place an ideal proving ground."

"Thank you, Doctor," says Harris Briggs.

"Just imagine," says Dr. Berglund, "if our work on radiation dosage levels could be performed directly on the target species instead of on laboratory surrogates."

"Gene splicing," says Dr. Rustafi.

"Infertility."

"*In utero* monitoring."

"I've long wanted," says Dr. Solomon, "to administer

extensive intelligence and personality integration bat-
teries to this population. The results should be ex-
tremely provocative."

"It occurs to me," says Dr. Harms, a sociologist, "that
any potential difficulties could be overcome by giving
the act of mating a ritual significance. Partners could be
selected and assigned, as work is. This would enable the
experimenters to assure that only the desired couplings
took place."

"Think what might be learned," says Dr. Lee, "if in
one out of every three cases, let's say, work was deliberately inappropriately assigned."

"Just so," cried Dr. Dixon. "The possibilities for environmental resource patch experimentation are almost
endless. Temporal, spatial, you name it. Almost any resource, physiological or psychological, could be artifi-
cially limited within the population."

"It would be a significant challenge," Dr. Stoller says,
"to reshape the language to include the concept of re-
production while divorcing it from the commonly negative aspects of sexual behavior, such as jealousy, por-
nography and promiscuity. On reflection, however, I
believe it could be done."

"You gentlemen begin to take my point," says Dr.
Kleig.

"The possibilities are limitless," says Harris Briggs,
"as long as our work continues to be funded."

"When science advances," says Kleig, "so too does
humankind."

"I find it shocking," says Dr. Allingham, "that so
many of you are so willing to consider what so obviously
amounts to a flagrant degradation of the principles of
our charter. And I'd like to hear what Dr. Halliburton
thinks of this."

"I oppose it," Alice says.

Dr. Allingham regards her sternly. "Is that all?"

"With every fiber of my being, I oppose it," Alice says. "Is that enough?"

"We should remember," Dr. Kleig says, "that of us all, Dr. Halliburton is least equipped to be objective on this point. Her emotional involvement in her work is bound to cloud her judgment."

"My judgment has guided the Place for sixteen years," Alice says.

Kleig nods acknowledgment. "Just so. You're to be commended for your long and dedicated service. I'm sure the rest of your colleagues will join me in feeling that your retirement is well-deserved."

"I have no plans to retire," Alice says.

"We're not letting her off the hook entirely," says Briggs. "We will continue to value and avail ourselves of the benefit of Dr. Halliburton's insight and experience. Though I'm sure that, in comparison to the rigors of the past sixteen years, your new responsibilities will seem quite light." Briggs makes a sweeping gesture. "Gentlemen, ladies, join me in honoring our colleague." He begins to clap. The whole Team rises to applaud her.

22

PETER COMES OF AGE. In some sense, the celebration redeems the loss of Leda, giving proof, as spring does after winter, that life goes on and is not devoid of incidental joys, and the People lay aside their grief to join it joyfully. Peter's metamorphosis is welcomed by beautiful and ingenious gifts. To these, the People open their senses, as flowers open to the sun, until the chill of sorrow becomes a memory, experienced and left behind.

Because of Bartholomew's intercession, and Brother Alice's, Peter's seven-fingered hand remains unchanged. When Bartholomew, in place of Brother Alice, gives Peter his work, which is to make music and teach the small ones to sing, Peter takes up his special instrument and says, "I want to play a new song. I made it for Bartholomew, who is wise and good."

Peter's song has two voices and two moods. The strings play a light and lilting melody, while the flute sings the same tune more slowly and in a minor key, transforming it to a lament. To Bartholomew, who feels neither wise nor good, the performance seems to iterate the dialogue his spirit carries on with itself and moves him to unwished for tears. With the camera, Ringer steals his sorrow, and Bartholomew sees his own weeping face many times enlarged, regarding him from each of the four walls.

It is two days and two nights since he has heard from Brother Alice. Clumsily, four times revealed, Bartholomew raises his flesh hand to wipe away his tears.

23

ALICE CLOSES HER FIST and raises it to knock, then hesitates. The corridor is quiet, no one is afoot at 3 A.M., what she fears is not being discovered, but what she might discover inside the room. Having reviewed all her colleagues, Alice has found only one from whom she might ask help and hope to get it, but now, outside Dorothy Allingham's door, she's seized with the sudden conviction that Kleig has gotten there before her, is inside right now and bodily conquering the foe. Kleig is a moaner, he comes with a wordless sound of deep release that she has heard three times. Waiting in the corridor, she expects to hear it a fourth.

No sound comes. Perhaps her real reluctance to knock is that knocking will commit her to a course of action, will turn her bitter daydream into a plan-in-execution. She makes herself knock. If Kleig's inside, so much the better; she'll spit in his eye, she'll malign his parentage, she . . .

The door opening disrupts her tirade and leaves her speechless. Night transforms the nutritionist, by day a creature who walks erect and oozes rectitude, into a peacock. Dorothy Allingham wears a turquoise dressing gown of Chinese silk, cinched in to reveal a curvature her daytime dresses hide; her disciplined French roll has been undone and her hair from crown to shoulders describes a wiry triangle. She draws Alice quickly into her room and shuts and bolts the door. The room is a mirror image of Alice's own—peach walls and stiff synthetic draperies that ape brocade. Here the prints are by Bonnard. Here, the window faces west.

When Alice finds her voice, it is to say, "I hope I didn't disturb you. If you're expecting someone, I'll go."

In previous encounters, Dorothy Allingham's features have never quite relinquished a look of real but understated disapproval. Now a smile cracks her rectitude and makes her human. "He's come and gone, my dear," she says.

"Kleig."

"Yes, Dr. Kleig came courting, or rather, lobbying. He found me quite unreceptive."

"You don't have to tell me," Alice says.

"There's nothing to tell. Except for one piece of information he did let fall, in hopes, I suspect, that I'd pass it on to you."

"What is it?"

"According to Dr. Kleig, Thomas Allworthy isn't dead."

"But I read his obituary. It said he died of coronary thrombosis."

"I saw that, too. But my visitor told me that Allworthy's kids had turned him antinuclear. He wanted to withdraw from the project. He's been lobotomized, Alice. Briggs got him a janitorial job at USC."

Alice notices that the false brocade bedspread is still pulled taut, the bed neatly made. She sits down on it. Dorothy Allingham stands in front of the dressing table so that Alice can see her back in the mirror as well as the concern on her face. "I don't know if it's true, of course," she says. "I do think it was meant to warn you."

"I came to ask your help," Alice says. "I have to get back to the Place."

"To pack your things?"

"To stay."

Dorothy Allingham unwinds a sigh. "What are you planning?"

Alice shakes her head, disclaiming foresight. "I need to be with the People," she says.

"I doubt very much that you can save them."

A sense of ritual makes Alice stand. Her eyes are drawn into the weave of Allingham's bathrobe, a terrain of turquoise dragons with claws poised to strike and bulging eyes. "Will you help me? Only to get out of here. I won't involve you further."

"What do you want me to do?"

"Distract the guard in the gatehouse. I can't make it over the chain-link fence. I've always been afraid of heights."

Dorothy Allingham searches her face closely, as if she hoped to find her answer in Alice's expression. At last she says, "I'll help, but not tonight. You need rest and you need a plan. Tomorrow night I'll help you."

"I can't afford to wait," Alice says.

"Of course you can. Sleep late, then join the conference. They'll think you've come around. You might learn something useful. And it'll give you a last chance to counteract the rumors that have begun to circulate."

"What rumors?"

"That you're dangerously unbalanced. A major security risk." Allingham smiles at her. "They're especially persuasive because so sympathetic. Poor Alice, living like that. No wonder. We should have seen it sooner. Things like that."

Allingham's eyes are a warm brown, stippled with flecks of cooler green. Alice watches them. "Do you think I'm unbalanced?"

The eyes smile; below, turquoise dragons twitch as Allingham shrugs. "Since I've designed your diet for the last sixteen years, I can vouch for *its* balance. You should be physically fit and as free of chemical poisons as it's humanly possible to be. I believe that correlates positively with good mental health." She laughs, and Alice wonders if she's ever heard her laugh before. "I wouldn't presume to answer philosophically," Allingham goes on. "That depends too utterly on whose scales you use. But if it's pathological to care deeply, then you're surely nuts."

Alice expected less equivocation, more reassurance. She needed it. *Tell me I'm right, I'm good, empower me. I will work miracles. Withhold faith and destroy me.*

"Of course, I think that everyone is nuts," Allingham amends. "In the absence of a uniform and coherent cultural standard, that's inevitably true."

Tell me I'm sane, I'm strong. The plea is silent. Tears gather in her eyes. Embarrassment can't stop them.

"I've agreed to help you," Allingham says. "I subscribe. Don't ask me to judge." She stands apart, tall and turquoise. Alice feels herself shrink, to the size of a single, particular body, her own. Nothing multiplies her power. Nothing can. There is no moral socket in which to plug herself, no universal current on which to draw. Her smallness is a kind of terror.

What she forecloses of cosmic certainty, Allingham redeems by compassion. She takes Alice by the hand, she seats her on the bed and gently wipes away her tears, then turns back the covers and helps her to lie down. When the lights are extinguished and the alarm clock set, Dorothy Allingham climbs in bed beside her and until she sleeps holds Alice in a loose embrace that is not sexual but merely human, the embrace of a parent or a friend, one small body of another in the dark.

Alice dreams of her mother until dawn.

24

"I'M COMING HOME," Brother Alice says.

Bartholomew grips the receiver tightly, as if to reinforce his hold on Brother Alice. "When?"

"I can't be sure. As soon as I can make it."

"The People will be glad to see you." Common sense tells him that a prodigal should not be met with grievances, but the memory of four days' silence still hurts, and he needs to speak of it. "I missed your calls. I worried," he says.

Brother Alice offers no apology. He says, "I have much to tell you about the Fathers."

"That's good. I have many questions."

"I need your help, Bartholomew."

The code, evoked, works quickly. "Of course."

"Listen closely. If anyone gets there before me, even if he says he comes from the Fathers, pay no attention to him. Tell him nothing. I am your Father now. Do you understand?"

"I understand your words," Bartholomew says. "I don't know what they mean."

"Good enough," Brother Alice says. "I'll explain when I get there. If I get there."

"When you get here," Bartholomew says.

There is a pause, then Brother Alice says, "If I don't, Bartholomew, do what you can for the People. Help them to honor the code, and remember that I loved you."

A click curtails Bartholomew's questions. Brother Alice is gone.

25

DOROTHY ALLINGHAM HOLDS out her wallet and her checkbook. "You'd better have these."

Alice hesitates to take them. Dorothy laughs. "Go on. My credit's excellent, and my signature's easy to forge. Just buy a used Datsun, not a Cadillac."

"I have money," Alice says.

"The point is, they won't be looking for me." Dorothy opens Alice's pocketbook and drops the wallet and the checkbook in it.

"You'll be implicated."

"I already am." Dorothy snaps the purse shut. "Mail them back to me when you're done. I hate canceling credit cards." Her smile dims and she puts her hand on Alice's shoulder. "Are you ready?"

It is impossible to be ready, but Alice is willing to make herself begin. She nods.

"All right, then." Dorothy opens the door and they emerge into the hallway. "We've had a few too many, remember?" She wavers slightly, deliberately, as they make their way toward the elevator. "As I was saying, Alice, I don't envy today's young women, believing they can have it all. Marriage, motherhood, career. What a burden. There's something to be said for making choices, like we did."

The elevator door opens. Dr. Dixon and Dr. Lee, bathrobed and sauna-bound, lean against the back wall. "Ladies." Dr. Dixon nods.

"Although," Dorothy says, "I will say that the Women's Movement *has* helped improve the single state considerably. These days if a male visitor is observed leaving my apartment after breakfast, it only enhances my reputation."

Alice laughs. The car descends. Dixon and Lee, though pretending not to listen, smile.

"The notched belt," says Dorothy, "is no longer the exclusive property of men. Haven't you found that?"

"I'm afraid that liberation has passed me by," Alice says. "I have a lot of catching up to do."

The men debark on two. "So far, so good," Dorothy says.

"I really *do* have a lot of catching up to do," Alice says.

The lobby is empty as they pass through it, though voices, male laughter, can be heard in the bar. The night outside is hot and hurts their lungs. Beyond the parking lot, where Kleig's Porsche awaits its master's touch, they leave the road and its lights to walk on the desert's hard parched skin. Their shoes awaken dust, little clouds that rise with each step, then settle. Dorothy holds Alice's arm, the pressure of her fingers communicates goodwill. When they come near the gatehouse, Alice crouches behind a tall cactus, casting no shadow, as Dorothy rejoins the road. Her "damn" rings out.

"Who's there?" a male voice, the voice of the guard, inquires. Alice hears his surprise, his wariness. Through the arms of the saguaro, she can see his flashlight challenge the darkness, can see his shadow stretch toward the road.

"Could you give me a hand?" Dorothy calls out to him. "I've broken the heel off my shoe." She hobbles toward the light. The guard leaves his post to assist her. "I tripped on a stone and turned my ankle." He trains his flashlight on the broken shoe.

Alice closes her eyes for the duration of a deep
breath, then, striking a compromise between fast and
quiet, makes for the gatehouse, where the road con-
stricts. As she passes through the funnel, she hears Dorothy laugh. "Can you imagine wearing such flimsy
shoes? Fashion makes fools of us all, I'm afraid."

Beyond the cyclone fence, Alice takes to the desert
again. Her own shoes are flat-heeled and sturdy. By
starlight, the shadow-mass of vegetation is gnarled and
otherworldly, the desert looks as if it should be cold, not
hot. The sound of her footsteps conjures others; small
feet scurry in the dust. A mile due west she finds the
highway. Dusty and sweating, she climbs on the shoulder and begins her vigil. Eastward, the darkness lifts a
little, a colorless lightening. For a long time, there is no
sound, and for a long time after she first hears the hum
of wheels, no vehicle appears. At last a miniature truck
takes shape on the horizon, growing slowly larger as it
approaches her.

She steps a foot or two into the road and sticks out her
mendicant thumb. Through the tinted windshield
glass, she tries to meet the driver's eyes and send her
message: I am harmless, I am desperate. The truck
passes her, then slows and stops. She runs after it and
climbs in.

The driver, middle-aged and balding, thighs wide on
the seat-bench, looks a little bit like Harris Briggs.
"Where you headed?" he asks.

"Wherever you are," Alice says.

The truck moves forward, and the driver takes his
eyes from the straight, flat road to study her. "Domestic
troubles," he diagnoses. "Am I right?"

Alice nods. "I couldn't take it anymore," she says.

26

IT'S STILL DARK, still early, his covers are warm, and at this hour, every image fits with every other. His editing principle is beautifully simple: things are the same, or they are different. This covers all cases. It explains everything. Conflict is only a special form of harmony, and paradox is aesthetically pleasing. The world and all things in it fall into place, and the tapes he edits now, imagined images laid on imaginary track, are the best he ever makes. He regrets only that he cannot keep or share them.

When a voice calls out on the intercom, "Bartholomew, come at once," he doesn't question it. He is either dreaming or he is not. He only dreams he dresses, in which case he is still warm in his bed, with nothing lost, or else he really dresses, really leaves his room, goes to the elevator and descends. It really doesn't matter to him which case is true. Outside, the wind feels too cold for a dream wind, the corrugation of the paths by frozen snow too rough for dream terrain, unless he is having a nightmare, but if it were a nightmare, then he should feel more fearful and less accepting than he does. The inner office is lighted but empty, a dream condition. The hands of the clock say it is 5:30 and that seems to him to be the correct time. The door without a knob opens. Brother Alice stands inside the doorframe, brightly silver. Bartholomew tries to alter the dream, to make it a giant crow inside the doorframe, or Leda, or no one at all, but Brother Alice persists. He says hello. Bartholomew says hello. He hears his own voice clearly, but he cannot see himself, as he sometimes can in dreams.

"Come with me," Brother Alice says. He pushes the door without a knob wide open and stands aside to let Bartholomew pass into a white hallway lined with white doors. He follows Brother Alice down the hall, past several closed doors, until they come to one on the end which stands open, and they enter it. Inside, a deep red carpet pushes against his wheels. He sees not one but two television sets, side by side, he sees red chairs and on a small glass table, under a lamp that gives off yellow light there is a picture of a face he seems to know, though he could not name its owner. Beyond this room there are others, but no light to reveal them. Once again he tries to change the course of the dream and once again cannot.

Brother Alice closes the door and goes to sit in a red chair. His scales reflect its redness. "It's good to see you," he says. "It's good to be home."

"Am I dreaming?" Bartholomew asks him.

Brother Alice smiles. "Not unless we're dreaming the same dream. These are my rooms. I missed the Place while I was gone."

"I missed you. We all did," Bartholomew says. "Will you miss the Fathers now?"

Brother Alice sighs. "I have a lot of things to tell you, Bartholomew. Not all of them are pleasant. Try to be patient and trust me."

She knows their hearts are weak and she fears his stopping, but the visual way seems best to her, the most direct and least ambivalent. He is a visual person. She stands and reaches for her inner zippers, opening her suit at the side from armpit to knee, freeing head from neck. Her arm emerges and holds the other until it, too, slides free. The suit is lightly elasticized under the scales and stretches to give her exit room. She lifts off the silver head and sets it on the red chair. As always, her hair is damp and her head itches from confinement. She pushes her wet bangs off her brow and looks at him. Pale, wide-eyed, but breathing. She steps out of the body of the suit and lays it, too, aside to stand before him in her leotard. In Bartholomew's tape, a swimming woman becomes a flying bird. Alice trusts his innate understanding of metamorphosis. She has to.

"Outside the Place, Bartholomew, there are many more people. In many ways, they're different from our People."

"I know," Bartholomew says. The apparition of Brother Alice stands before him, two-armed, two-legged, diminished by the loss of his scales. His black garment does not reflect the light but absorbs it, his face and hands are small and pallid. Bartholomew feels sorrow at this transformation, but no surprise. "There are other people who are the same on both sides," he says. "Their eyes and ears are level and they are like each other."

It is Brother Alice who seems surprised. "How do you know?"

"For a long time, I watched the insects and the birds and suspected it. Then a tape came from the Fathers."

"The Fathers sent a tape?"

"The tape came in a box of blanks. It was imperfectly erased. We could still make out the images of people running. Those people were like each other. They were the same on both sides."

"Do the others know?"

"Only Ringer. Ringer is angry. He wants to know why."

"And you?" Brother Alice asks.

And he. Bartholomew respects the power of knowledge as he respects the power of the elements. He would prefer to have learned nothing, to have spent his life in idle speculation, watching birds, but it's clear to him that half-knowledge, knowing at once too much and not enough, is the least desirable estate of all, and he eschews it. "I want to know," he says.

She has her wish. His slate is hers to fill, his innocence awaits corruption, but what he lacks she was almost born knowing, drank with her mother's milk, acquired with language, absorbed from the electrons glowing on the television screen, from printer's ink on wood pulp, she learned at home, in school, from the water and the air. Before she could read, she knew of human nature, she knew about power and greed and coitus and the Bomb. Thousands of years of history, of progress and retrenchment, lie between them. Where to begin?

The gene and the atom—these seem to be the essential and irreducible ideas. If she can make him understand these, the rest will come. Both ideas seem simple only because their history is complex, only because the idea is most commonly understood in the context of the quest for the idea, and Alice has neither the time nor the will to take him on those journeys, cannot recapitulate the history of science for his benefit, but must present ideas as facts, ultimate and irrefutable as the mysteries are. New mysteries. She will not tell him that they are only resting places along the way, ideas awaiting revision.

She begins with the gene because as an idea it seems more palpable to her, more relevant and congenial, somehow, than atoms; others, she knows, would debate her choice. On blank paper, she draws a double helix, then unwinds it for him. She explains sequence, and the importance of sequencing, sets the messenger RNA to work and develops a cartoon embryo to parturition. Much is, of necessity, left out; the period of gestation, from conception to birth, takes place inside an hour. Alice is aware that she could not defend her thesis; she's glad he's not yet mastered the art of doubting.

The atom next. She creates it, a kind of Everyatom, on a virgin sheet of paper, sets electrons circling its penciled nucleus, then sends them leaping shell to shell. She creates the atom, then splits it, releasing its terrible power. It seems to her that she is speaking poetry, that what she gives him is more metaphor than truth, more symbol than science, and yet, almost unbelievably, it works, can be applied. Hiroshima is vaporized, Pennsylvania is lighted, Bartholomew has no legs.

"Do you have any questions?" Brother Alice asks him.

The figures that Brother Alice draws for him represent power, yet in themselves they have no power—Bartholomew understands that much well enough. But this level of abstraction, where the assignment of significance to symbol is admittedly arbitrary, is new to him, and he finds it hard to keep the pictures invested with their rightful meanings through the long and complicated story that Brother Alice tells him. He would like to ask a question worthy of his teacher's effort, but it is too soon. He shakes his head. No.

Cause and effect next. Now she must relate the two ideas. Now she must corrupt and complicate the empty purity of science with human motivations. Power, greed, politics. These notions are difficult for him, even though they catalyzed his own condition and continue to define his life. She invokes evil, she brings it into being in his mind, and finds herself hoping that propensity does not exist in him, awaiting definition.

Once again, Brother Alice asks him for questions, and Bartholomew senses that the only proper question—why?—is beyond even Brother Alice's power to answer it. His new strange face is pale and looks tired, his light voice searches for words and sometimes trips on them. Bartholomew believes that Brother Alice is doing his best. Still, he wants to offer proof of his attentiveness, to show his teacher that he, too, has worked hard. He needs a question to betoken love.

There was one point earlier he found confusing at the time. What was it? He tries to reconstruct the genetic anecdote, until he isolates the place the plot turned hazy. "Something about the chromosomes," he says. Bartholomew shuffles through pages of crude diagrams until he finds the one that puzzled him. The new vocabulary is not yet fixed in his mind, so he speaks what he sees: How does one ball get two sets of worms?

Brother Alice laughs, not unkindly, and his pale cheeks seem to pinken as he laughs.

Alice takes a deep breath. The outer limits of pedagogy have been attained. "You mean, by what mechanism?"

"I guess so."

"You remember I told you all these things take place within the body?"

Bartholomew nods.

"So the problem becomes transporting genetic material from one body to another."

"I think that's my question," Bartholomew says. "I don't understand how that happens."

Alice studies him closely for a moment, the perfect

innocence of his green eyes, features both fine and strong as Donatello's *David*'s, the androgynous fall of light brown hair that always seems startling in contrast to the redness of his beard. "I am not your brother," Alice says. "There is a necessary difference even between those who are the same." She tugs at the neckline of her leotard until one shoulder, then both are exposed, until her body is revealed to him. "Do you see, Bartholomew?"

Brother Alice shows him and he sees, he feels, he knows and once he knows, knows too that nothing will ever be the same again. They share the Excitement. Nature intended that the Excitement should be shared. He is not dreaming.

27

IT COMES AMID a thin sheaf of Christmas greetings. The top envelope is dimpled with the imprint of snowflakes melted then dried when she takes her mail from William's ungloved hand. Only one letter is of interest to Alice. Its return address reads: *Nuclear Regulatory Commission, Office of the Director.*

It says:

Dear Dr. Halliburton:

I hope this finds you feeling better.

Your hasty departure from last week's convocation of the Team I take as a manifestation of the intense stress of your situation. I reproach myself, as your superior, for having been so long insensitive to your condition.

This is to advise you, therefore, that your employment ends in two weeks' time. You will continue to receive three quarters of terminating salary and full medical and dental benefits for the remainder of your life. If, after a period of rest and recuperation, you find you would like to pursue your work, this office would be pleased to help you secure an appropriate academic appointment.

Dr. Kleig and his staff will arrive in fifteen days to relieve you of your duties. Your final assignment is to prepare the inmates for the new administration. I know you will execute your responsibilities faithfully now as in the past.

Seasons greetings,
Harris E. Briggs

28

"BROTHER ALICE IS DIFFERENT NOW," Ringer says.

For Bartholomew, Brother Alice, having shed skins twice, is doubly transformed. It is hard to understand Ringer's observation only in Ringer's terms. "How so?" he asks.

"He no longer tells us what to do," Ringer says.

It's true. With his silver scales, Brother Alice has taken off some part of his magic, too. The new magic he offers in its place is dark and frightens Bartholomew. He says, "I know."

Ringer laughs at his gravity. "You miss what's gone."

Bartholomew sees no humor in what feels like loss but, seeing that Ringer does, he smiles. "You love what's new."

"I love *knowing*," Ringer says.

"We know more facts and fewer truths," Bartholomew corrects. "At least I do."

But Ringer will not trim his sails for his old master. His grin seems to Bartholomew almost indecently delighted.

"It's like making a tape," Ringer says. "You add new images, more and more, until the collection of images becomes a single image."

Bartholomew envies Ringer his easy conviction that information necessarily acquires meaning. He envies Ringer's appetite for meaning. Brother Alice defrocked seems singular and vulnerable as any of the People and Bartholomew finds him both easier and harder to love. He is uncomfortable inside the paradox. "What if each collection of images is only one image in a bigger collection?" he asks Ringer.

Bartholomew feels as if he is being sucked through the lens. The zoom is smooth and slow, he is bound to the lever and has no choice but to ride it out.

Ringer laughs at his question. "So be it," he says.

29

ALICE IS OF THE PEOPLE. She is. As one of the People, she has her work, and having work is different from doing a job. Her work is to educate the People, to guide without steering, to enable them. She is no longer an autocrat but a democrat. No longer leader, she becomes advisor, her knowledge a resource of the People, as Lucas's voice is, or Boris's ingenuity. She sees that new work requires new morality, and she tries to apply the code to her practice. It insists on neutrality, that she seek a lucid compromise between realities.

"Do the people outside live by the code?" Ringer asks her. "If we ask them for their help, will they give it?"

What is the answer? The code was born outside but can't survive there. The people outside follow many different codes. Some few—how few?—people outside live by our code. Of these, some few—how few?—might believe the code applies to us, to the People. Of these, how many would be willing to act in our behalf? How few? Perhaps just one lone person. Perhaps none.

Nuance builds a maze whose core is hard to find. The truth is, she has no idea what is true.

"I don't know," she tells Ringer. Her intellect requires that answer. Her intuition is slightly more sanguine. "It's not impossible," she lets her hope amend.

All of this makes it both easier and more difficult for her to love Bartholomew.

30

THE STRANDS OF THE HELIX are blue and green. Through a trick of perspective, Clotho's, they appear three dimensional, a corkscrew suspended in deep space. Remaining parallel, they unwind, they become two straight lines that do not touch. This flattens the blackness. One image dissolves into another, and the lines become strung beads. There is pattern but no uniformity in the way the beads are strung. There are repetitions, but the repetitions are too small and too isolated to reveal a master strategy.

Alice measures the sequence against what she knows of the scientific paradigm. "It looks all right to me," she says.

Clotho admires the elegance of the design. The images are Nature's. Brother Alice evoked them, he re-created them. To see them move extends his sense of possibility, it pleases his eye.

The easel is tilted subtly to discourage shadows and to cut glare. A camera, tripod-stabilized, trains on the drawing. Counting, Ringer shoots. Two three four. He stops shooting, takes the drawing from its mount and carefully replaces it with another, of the helix a hairsbreadth less tightly wound. Two three four. It requires many drawings, each slightly different, consecutively photographed in perfect register, to make visual what takes place, in Nature, beyond seeing. The process of making visual is painstaking and slow, a matter of patient craft.

It works. As Bartholomew plays the edited tape on the monitor, the individual images become continuous, they twine and separate and are transformed. The eye is tricked, the brain is fooled. No pauses, and the rhythm of the dance, Ringer's four/four time, is imperceptible. Bartholomew believes he watches a mystery unfolding.

RECORD.

Collaboration requires argument. Bartholomew finds it hard to disagree with Brother Alice, hard not to defer to him, even when the idea he advances is less good than another. In technical matters, Brother Alice always defers to him or to Ringer. Once or twice, he says something so naïve about television that without thinking, Bartholomew and Ringer laugh. Brother Alice does not seem to mind being laughed at. He is willing to laugh at himself. Bartholomew remembers the shared Excitement. On the screen, satellite particles swim complex orbits around a purple nucleus. On the track, Brother Alice talks about energy, about power.

SYNC.

It is a delicate business to work with Bartholomew. He's shy to claim his expertise and slow to accept her nonauthority. She wishes his reticence, his habit of respect were something he could simply remove, as easily as clothes. When he forgets to be humble and lets himself be seduced by his own deep enthusiasm for the medium, when he forgets she is watching and takes charge of his tools or dares to laugh when she asks a foolish question, then Alice sees the person she would have him be, and is encouraged. Removing her silver suit before the camera, repeating for all the People the revelation only one has shared, Alice feels strangely shy herself.

RUN IT.

In their rooms, on their televisions the People watch two-legged two-armed symmetrical people, people whose eyes are level, whose bodies seem to have been manufactured in a single, common mold pursue each other endlessly around a flattened circle. The picture is snowy, less sharp than pictures Bartholomew and Ringer take, but the message is clear: there are people outside the Place. They are different from us.

A fade erases them and for a moment the screen is dark, then from blackness emerges the silver countenance of Brother Alice. As the People watch, he peels away his silver skin, revealing flesh and symmetry. "I too once lived outside," he tells them.

Brother Alice tells them that the Place is in danger. He weaves a story of many strands, of the perfidy of the Fathers and the ignorance of the people outside, to explain to them why this should be so. Because the story is well-told, because order inheres in the telling and because they trust the medium, the People are willing to believe it, and for a moment, share the illusion of whole cloth, before their questions begin to ravel the edges of the story fabric.

"You must have many questions," Brother Alice says. "I will try to answer them. Please understand that my answers are not necessarily the best answers, or the only answers to your questions."

The People's questions push upstream, to the studio where Alice waits. Peter's face appears on the monitor, and on the screens of the People. His voice asks, *Why have the Fathers set us apart from the others? If we are like them, why can't we live together?*

The Fathers believe that the people outside fear what is different from themselves. The Fathers believe that you would frighten the people outside and that in their fear, they might come to oppose the will of the Fathers.

Lucas asks, *How do the Fathers think of us?*

The Fathers are willing to experiment with your bodies and your minds. Their code does not permit them to
experiment with the people outside.

Why do the Fathers want to experiment with us?

They want to learn what will happen to people if they
make a nuclear war. Also, they are curious.

What is war?

War is the intentional destruction of one group of
people by another.

Why do people make war?

I don't know.

Your answer is insufficient.

As I understand it, there are several reasons. One, to
prove they are strong. Two, to prove they are right.
Three, because one group of people wants what another group of people has. Four, because it excites
them. Five, because making and using the tools of war
makes work for people. War is good for the economy.

What is the economy?

The economy is the code of the people outside.

Explain, please.

It would take me a long time to explain. We would be
up all night.

How would the experiments of the Fathers hurt us?

They would take your time. They would bring you
pain and frustration.

*Don't we owe the Fathers something in return for the
fullness of our lives?*

Do we owe them the fullness of our lives?

Will the Fathers be angry if we resist them?

Yes.

*What will happen to Brother Alice if he is taken from
us?*

He will no longer be Brother Alice.

Is this how the Fathers reward service to them?

Sometimes, when they are frightened.

How do we know that we can trust Brother Alice?

You don't know that. Trust is believing without knowing.

Why has Brother Alice lived among us for so long?

Because he loves you. Are you ready to decide?

There are more questions.

There will always be more questions.

What does Brother Alice want us to do?

I want you to decide. I will abide by your decision.

Will the people outside help us?

I can't promise that they will. I am of them, and I would help us. I hope they will help us.

Why?

I don't know why. Are you ready to decide?

Please state our choices.

One. You can accept the will of the Fathers. Brother Alice will be removed from the Place. The Fathers will come instead. Your lives will be changed profoundly.

Two. You can attempt to resist the will of the Fathers. To do this, you must attempt to enlist the help of the people outside. You must let them know of your existence. You must ask them to influence their leaders to let the Place survive.

Your lives will change profoundly.

Do you have questions?

How will we make ourselves known to the people outside?

Through television. Television is the universal communication tool of the people outside. Are you ready to decide?

We are not ready, but we will decide.

VOTE.

The options are encoded RED and GREEN. GREEN is to give in. RED is to resist. Each in his own room, on

his own unit, the People choose. Almost instanta-
neously, the computer in the system tallies their responses.

REPORT.

On each screen in every room, an asterisk flashes red.
The People have chosen to resist.

31

BROTHER ALICE HAS LIT them by a distant candle, a
small ellipsoid sun whose concentric diffusions both
hide and reveal them. Bartholomew's eyes are avid and
shy. He looks at Brother Alice and thinks of birds, he
tries to imagine that pale symmetry in flight. Darkness
abets illusion. Squinting into the candlelight, letting the
flame smash like a star filter, Bartholomew almost suc-
ceeds in making Brother Alice fly.

Neither of them has spoken for a long time. The
silence is Brother Alice's, and Bartholomew is content
to respect it. Brother Alice's fingertips move back and
forth along his flipper, alternately smoothing and startling the fine hairs that grow from his skin until that
part speaks for him, becomes him. Bartholomew is his
flipper, and his flipper is big as the darkness that surrounds them, as bright as stars.

Still.

Still another part of him stands back to watch and to
record. He recognizes such intensity of touching. It is
his own, the reverence of his flesh hand on the fine
mechanism of the camera, the curiosity of his skin in
contact with the textures of his world. His hand knows
the splintery abrasion of bark on a tree stem, the waxy
smooth of leaves. So Brother Alice studies him, and
Bartholomew wonders if he is worth knowing so well.

It occupies her, touching him. She anchors her senses
at the meeting place of skins. Touch helps to dispel the
strangeness of his mutant body. Regarded discretely
enough, touched long enough, his flipper loses the
power to shock her. His flipper becomes beautiful. Alice touches him intently, minutely, to rectify the big-

otry of her aesthetic expectations, her prejudice of form. Educating, reporting and learning to accept, her fingers journey him.

Terra incognita.

Bartholomew.

The first time they were together, Alice found herself diffident of his female part. Her eyes evaded it, she did not touch, instead, concentrated her attention on his maleness. Later, alone, she regretted her circumspection. Bartholomew is composed of two parts. This time (so hard to be alone, so rare) she is determined to love all of him. By touch she finds the gristly rose between his petals, she looks at the nub and whorls and ridges of his flesh, at the dusky-sunset-colored channel and the deep canal, until she can look at them without embarrassment. Can touch them lovingly. What his body does in response—arch, squeeze, spasm—is familiar to her as her own face in the mirror, and as much a revelation.

His maleness, unrequited, looks on. Must experience style her always the aggressor? Alice wishes he would touch her. On his own initiative, by his own volition. She doesn't want to instruct him. She doesn't want to have to ask.

Arch squeeze spasm

For a moment, Bartholomew flies, is borne on wings of light through blackness, where the winds blow fast but surprisingly warm and the drag of gravity is only a friction that enhances the pleasure of soaring.

Lift circle stabilize

Touch me, Brother Alice says.

The wind carries his voice, up up, a small voice riding the wind. It reaches Bartholomew, it summons him and he begins his descent, down cool shafts in the blackness, sometimes catching an updraft, rising with it, sometimes in freefall. The cool softness of Brother Alice cushions his drop.

Touch me.

Bartholomew's flesh hand feels ignorant and crude, shy of the mystery of Brother Alice, unwilling to offend or hurt him. Yet he is licensed to explore. At first his touchings are small and tentative, but Brother Alice is patient while he gains confidence and, finally, courage. With blind daring, Bartholomew mounts the twin round ridges of Brother Alice's legs, he travels flesh and what he finds at journey's end, at the confluence of symmetrical flesh limbs, is a fault line like his own.

Come, Brother Alice says. Come in.

Bartholomew's second self joins with her only

he she him her his hers

they them their

we us our

32

"TEN DAYS."

Alice waits as each makes his own conversion between personal time and the Fathers' arbitrary grid of hours and days. For Clotho, time is measured in paintings. How long it takes to mix constituent hues into a color that evokes the color of a winter sky and what it feels like to be alive under that sky is a standard, valid unit of Clotho-time. To Louis, a day is the cycle of meals prepared and served between a single waking and its paired sleep. The tools and processes of video mark Bartholomew's and Ringer's time. Alice-time is a paradoxical substance: the fixed blocks of days, marbled with urgency and impossibility; the flow of a river into whose currents she casts herself.

"Ten days," Boris repeats. He says the words as if they were objects he could touch and turn in his hands.

Alice nods. She recapitulates. "Bartholomew and Ringer will make a census of the People. They will leave the Place and take their tapes to the makers of television outside. We'll stockpile food and supplies, enough to be self-supporting for as long as possible. Boris and Clotho will help me prepare a plan to neutralize the Fathers when they come. All this," she says, "in ten days' time."

Ringer is quick to learn the Fathers' units and to perform the inversion necessary to use them to measure action. "It will take us two days to shoot and edit the tape if we both work steadily."

Bartholomew looks at him. "You leave no time for sleeping."

"There is no time for sleeping," Ringer says. "Don't worry. There will be time to stop and eat."

"When the messengers come, I'll order enough food for many meals," Louis says.

"Boris?" Alice says. The inventor's eyes wear the glaze that means he's seeing inward; his lips, moving slightly, seem to mirror the motion of his thoughts. When Alice calls him, the blind lifts and he looks outward. "First I have to pursue the idea," he explains. "If I catch it quickly enough, there will be time to make it happen. If the idea comes slow . . ." He shrugs.

So easy with his own modes of working, Boris seems immune to pressure, and Alice wonders fleetingly what management techniques IBM or General Electric would use to make him conform to corporate deadlines, what seductions to make him satisfy the corporate desire. The only incentive she has to offer is survival. "The idea won't come slow," she says. "It can't."

"Our gifts are always ready when one of the People comes of age," Bartholomew says. "This is no different."

It is different and they all know it, but Boris nods thanks for the metaphor. "I will think of my task as a gift," he says.

Clotho, who has been silent, watching and listening, speaks from his cart. "I don't understand what help I can give. I think I paint well, I like my paintings very much, but I know too that paintings are powerless."

Brother Alice, who is not silver now but made of flesh, of pale flesh brittled by fatigue, smiles at him. "Vision is not powerless, Clotho, nor is imagination."

As he speaks, Brother Alice moves his head a little to the right so that the lamplight which revealed him becomes a kind of goldish nimbus around his shadowed face. His fatigue, the fallibility of his flesh are no longer visible, but only the shine of his eyes, which seem to generate, without reflection, a special light. Clotho watches, and believes he witnesses a transformation: of authority to power, from posited abstraction to operant truth. This is the vision he experiences, and he accepts it.

Bartholomew is without visions; the light, from where he sits, has no pity. The clean geometry of Brother Alice's profile is marred by worry, is made eccentric by sleeplessness and by the weight of the burdens he undertakes to bear. Bartholomew does not question the role he is to assume, only the reason he must assume it. He does not want to leave the Place, he would rather merge with Brother Alice than be separated from him. It seems wrong to him he should be sent away, he would like to protest his banishment, but knows his arguments would seem selfish. "We understand our assignments," he says. "We will do our best."

Alice hears his sadness and knows it is her bitter gift. Had she not taught him love, there would be no pain at separation. At the same time, it is a gift she has received as well as given, she is as compromised as he. She looks at Bartholomew, at his emphatic features and fine unworldly eyes, and feels a tenderness as sharp as lust.

"Ten days." Ringer, speaking aloud, speaks for them all.

33

WHEN RINGER MOVES close to the cradle, camera shouldered, the nestling Ione begins to howl. His skin darkens, his eyes puff shut, his face becomes all mouth for better howling. Bartholomew, watching, is ungenerously pleased to find there are still holes in Ringer's expertise. "Babies are like birds," he says. "You have to stalk them."

Ringer backs away from the cradle and swings the camera down unsmiling.

"Imagine what you look like to him," Bartholomew says. "You'd be frightened, too."

Ringer holds out the camera. "You do it, then."

"I'll help you," Bartholomew says. He moves close to the cradle, lowers its side and lifts the nestling onto his lap. He makes soft clucking noises with his tongue, he bounces the little body gently up and down until its bawling becomes provisional, then stops altogether. "Will you sing with me, Ione? You sing with me. Let's sing." He varies the bouncing with sways from side to side. "That's it, Ione. Let's sing." His lullaby is made of nonsense sounds, la la loo loo, its tune impromptu. Ione watches Bartholomew's eyes, then his lips. Soon he tries his own voice, cooing, pleased and startled by the sounds he makes.

Silent and smoothly, Ringer slips behind them and, over Bartholomew's shoulder, shoots. The baby, playing, takes no note of him. "Done," he says. "I got it." Bartholomew lifts the baby high in the air above his head, arms and flippers kicking, before he lays him back in the cradle and secures its side.

Ringer is silent as they move on to the next infant, but

when they arrive at cribside, says, "Go ahead. You might as well play with this one, too."

The nestling gurgles a greeting as Bartholomew lifts him up. "Sometimes," he says to Ringer, "to waste time is to save it."

Among the older children, the census is easier to make. Bartholomew explains that each of them will have his turn before the camera, that each must say his own name for the tape. He patches the camera into the playroom's television set so the small ones can see their pictures on the screen. Some are solemn, others giggle and make faces at the camera. Their voices, reproduced, are high and clear. Last of all, they photograph Joseph in his bed.

After lunch they fix the cameras on tripods in the dining hall, and one by one the People pass before them, telling their names and their work:

I am Adolph, the gymnast.

My name is Louis. I cook the People's food.

I am Lupe. I make sculptures.

The limbless are wheeled before the camera. *I am Clotho, the painter.*

The blind are led there, and seated on a stool. "Speak to my voice," Bartholomew tells them. *I am Susanna. I wash the People's clothes.*

The voiceless tell their names and work in the language of hands, while Bartholomew repeats their messages into the microphone. *I am Marco. I keep the paths and lawns.*

At first, Beatrice is grave in front of the camera; then, in the flicker of an instant, his expression becomes a parody of gravity, and Bartholomew and Ringer laugh out loud at the change. Their laughter becomes part of the tape. *I am Beatrice, the mime.*

Lucas's bright, bubbling cylinder is rolled in place,

and the camera pans up, up to see his face. *I am Lucas.
My voice is the voice of the People.*

*I am Boris, the inventor. I make new tools and new
toys.*

My name is Ernestine. I make up plays.

I am Dorian, the keeper of the pool.

I am Pavlova, a photographer.

*I am Peter. I make up songs and play them on the
instrument that Boris built for me.*

*My name is Fabian. I care for the flowers and the
shrubs.*

I am Ruth, the weaver.

Technically, the task is simple and repetitious—body
shot, close up, body shot, close up—but Bartholomew
doesn't find it boring. In the course of the afternoon and
evening, all of the People pass before his lens or
Ringer's, and though he knows the tape cannot expose
his love for them, he feels it deeply. Many of the People
linger after their turn is done to watch their friends
before the cameras, so that work becomes event, an
occasion for the examination of the collective self, to
which the cameras contribute both dignity and objec-
tivity.

At last, all the People but two are counted. Ringer
stands before the camera. In the viewfinder, his winter-
long fur is dark, grainy gray; his face, when Bartholomew zooms in, is white. *I am Ringer, a maker of television.*

They trade places, and Bartholomew feels, as all the
People before him have, the self-conscious excitement
of being subject. The stare of the lens unsettles him, his
heart is pounding, and this makes him smile. *I am Bartholomew,* he says. *I, too, make television.*

34

THE CEILING IS FLAT, light-consuming blackness, the air surrounding them, their ambience, a delicate light-passing black. In darkness, they have no shape but are only voices, two thin and different voices jumping the brief, immeasurable chasm between their bodies.

Is it really possible, he asks, to stop being of the Fathers and to start being of the People?

Yes, she tells him. I am where my commitment is. No, she tells him, because they are still a part of me. I can still imagine their perceptions. I can state their arguments. Their arguments that I'm crazy are good.

What is crazy? he asks.

Unable to choose between realities, I suppose. What they don't understand is that I've chosen. That means I'm sane.

Not crazy?

Sane is the opposite of crazy. I'm not crazy. Beyond the pale, but not crazy.

I'm confused, he tells her. The Place is good, but the things that led to the Place were not good.

No.

Why didn't you oppose them?

I ask myself that often. My lens was not political.

I don't understand political.

I wasn't thinking of the greater good. It was a rare opportunity. I thought only of myself.

You're not thinking of yourself now.

Yes and no. I could no longer live in their world. I'd be a freak.

Freak?

I no longer conform to their symmetries. It would be as obvious to them as if I wore my silver suit.

You fear that?

Also you're here. That I can love you says that I'm of you. I belong here. Otherwise I would not love. It's something like speciation.

His silence questions, and she sighs. Like birds, she tells him. A crow can mate with another crow but not with a hummingbird. There'll never be a humming-crow. Nature does more than prohibit, she prevents.

Mate?

To combine genetic material. To do the dance of DNA. To share the Excitement, she tells him. To love.

Love.

Don't set too much stock in the word. Trust the feeling.

I'm just beginning to learn to match the word to the feeling.

So am I.

Why must I go away?

Because you must.

You speak as before, when there were no questions.

All right. You have to go because I'm afraid to send one of you alone. Because you and Ringer are two of the more relatively normal-looking People. Because you use language well and should be able to communicate with the makers of television outside. Also, you have to go to help me prove my own sincerity to myself. You have to help me prove that my convictions are stronger than my passions.

You use words I don't know.

To prove that I love the People more than I love myself. Or you.

Why do you have to choose?

When one assumes responsibility, choice becomes

necessity. I have accepted a position whose demands are more important than my own happiness. It is more important that the Place survive than that Alice should be happy. Do you understand?

I think so.

It's my turn to ask questions.

Unless you want to ask about television, I don't have many answers. I could teach you to take pictures of birds, or to dissolve between two images.

I'd like that. Why are you here?

I'm here because you called me.

Did you want to come?

Yes.

Did you want to come more than you wanted to be in the studio with Ringer?

Yes.

Would you have come if I hadn't called you?

No.

Why not?

Because I would have thought you didn't want me to come.

What about what you wanted?

When you were gone to the Fathers, I wanted you to come back to the Place. I was impatient waiting for your calls.

That's something. I want you to want to be with me. Do you understand?

I understand. It's easier to understand than to believe.

Believe. But later. Now you should sleep. I've kept you up too long. Your adventure begins before dawn.

It's a long time before dawn.

Not long enough. Sleep now. Put your head on my shoulder. There. Sleep.

Brother Alice?

Yes, Bartholomew?

When I'm gone from the Place, I'll want to be with you.

I'll want to be with you. My thoughts will be with you.

What will happen to us on the outside?

I don't know. Sleep.

When you tell the People what to do, do you know you're right in what you tell them?

I usually think I am. Not always. Sometimes I guess.

I would rather spend the time before dawn awake than sleeping.

Do you want to go someplace else? If you want to be alone, I understand. Would you rather be with Ringer?

I want to be awake and I want to be here. Do you understand?

I do. And so do I.

35

SIX BROAD CONCRETE STEPS spread like a skirt around the entrance to the television station, and Bartholomew can appreciate their efficiency, that the stacking of angles makes it possible to attain elevation in less space than the gentler angle of a continuous incline would allow. A simple, elegant geometry, yet insurmountable. His round wheels cannot climb it, his chair lacks the power to leap those edges or to overcome the inertia gravity exerts. As Brother Alice drove them to the city, through the lens-like windows of his car, the world outside appeared to Bartholomew as a hectic panoramic dream, an infinity of discontinuous images made continuous by the motion that approached, juxtaposed them for an instant, left them behind. Now all the outside world is focused in a single image, one that subsumes all others: six neat perpendiculars, cruel in their uniform simplicity.

Ringer's hand on his shoulder condoles. Ringer, with his working limbs, could subdue those angles, he could climb the stairs. For a moment, for the first time, Bartholomew perceives an inequality between them.

"There has to be another way," Ringer says. "Remember, Brother Alice said their law requires it. I'll look."

He leaves Bartholomew at the foot of the stairs and follows a cement path that takes him out of sight, past a small planting of ornamental shrubs, around the side of the building. As Bartholomew waits for him, several people approach the station and mount the stairs. They step around his chair, their symmetrical bodies acknowledge the space he occupies, but they are careful not to look at him, they do not meet his eyes. Bartholomew watches their climbing, sees how their legs, rising, imitate the angle of the stairs in an unconscious synchrony, and feels a sympathetic tingle in his lower limbs, as if they understood the feel of rise and stretch or from some faded dream remembered it.

Ringer appears at the corner of the building and motions him to come. Setting his chair in motion, Bartholomew mimics the sharp turn of the path. The cement strip is scarcely wider than the span of his wheels, and he takes care not to slip off and mar the bordering garden beds.

"This way," Ringer says. "I found the sign that Brother Alice told us about."

They cross a stretch of concrete filled with cars and then Bartholomew sees it, a small blue rectangle rimmed in white. The blue is improbable, the blue of no sky he has ever seen, not Nature's blue. Against it, on it, is the crude and simple drawing of a person in a wheelchair. Shown in profile, the figure has a round, unfeatured head and only one set of visible limbs—one arm, one leg. The sign is affixed to the building, beside a wide door. Ringer holds the door open while Bartholomew wheels himself inside.

They enter a long corridor just wheelchair wide. From the open doors which line it, sounds reach them —human voices speaking, the sound of human voices electronically reproduced. Several different musics escape the rooms to mingle in the hallway. Below unintelligible letters, an arrow points to their right, and they follow it. In the rooms as they pass them, Bartholomew catches glimpses of editors and monitors, machines he knows, of people he doesn't know absorbed in work like his. For the hundredth time in one short morning, he has the sense of having landed wakeful in one of his own dreams. He does not entirely trust the dreamer. Ringer behind him picks one of the motifs from the music-laden air and whistles it. Bartholomew holds tightly to the tape-filled leather case on his lap to steady it, to keep his hand from trembling.

The corridor delivers them to a room on their left. The room is large, filled with chairs and plants. Not just the hall but several doors lead to it. A person surrounded by machines sits at a big wood desk and Bartholomew knows from the tapes he's watched, from Brother Alice's instruction, that the person is a person of Brother Alice's sex, a female. The hair is long, the features fine. When the person lifts his face to them, Bartholomew sees it has been painted—the lips bright red, the eyelids blue. The pink of hard exercise, of a chairball game or water dance, sits on his cheeks, but his breathing is shallow and Bartholomew does not believe he's been exercising.

For a moment before he smiles, the person simply looks at them. "May I help you?"

"We'd like to see the leader of the studio, please," Bartholomew says. He says it with courtesy, with dignity.

The person laughs. "That's good. I'll have to remember that. Do you have an appointment?"

"No."

"What are your names?"

"Bartholomew," Bartholomew says.

"Ringer."

"Mr. Bartholomew and Mr. Ringer. And who do you represent?"

"We make television."

"I see. Okay, I'll call his secretary."

The person pushes buttons on a telephone console and speaks low into the mouthpiece. When he hangs up, he says, "The station manager's schedule is very tight today. This is ratings week. It might be better if you made an appointment to come back toward the end of next week."

"It's important that we see him as soon as possible," Bartholomew says. "We have some tapes to show him. We're willing to wait."

This time appraisingly, the person looks at them. "Are you guys with the Veterans Video Project, by any chance? The one that's been interviewing all the Vietnam vets?"

"No," Ringer says.

"I see." Again, the person uses the telephone, hangs up. "Well, his secretary knows you're here. She can't promise he'll have time to see you."

"We'll wait."

"Have a chair then," the person says. He looks at Bartholomew, and his cheeks grow pinker.

Bartholomew maneuvers his chair into a space against the wall where no chair is. Ringer sits beside him. A large television screen mounted in the back wall is on, though no one watches it. Laughter, the sound of multitudes laughing, spills from the track. A person dressed in gray, clutching a microphone, spins a large red and black wheel. The wheel clicks as it spins, comes slowly to rest. A high voice shrieks.

"I think they're playing some kind of game," Ringer whispers.

The picture changes to rows of people sitting in chairs. Their seats are not tiered, so only their faces can be seen, dozens of like faces, two eyes, two ears, a protruding nose, a single mouth. Bartholomew wonders if he could ever learn to tell so many similar faces apart, to say with confidence, this is Clotho, this is Leda, this is Joseph. All the faces smile at the camera, and then the people are gone, replaced by a picture of a plastic bottle. A cartoon person lifts the cap and emerges from the bottle, flexes cartoon muscles and sings a song about cleanliness.

One game replaces another on the television set. The red-lipped person rises from his desk and asks if they'd like coffee.

"Yes," Ringer says.

When the person leaves the room, Bartholomew asks Ringer what coffee is.

"I don't know," Ringer says.

Coffee is a beverage, dark brown and bitter-tasting. It's hot, a rich and bitter-smelling steam rises from it. The cup that holds it warms Bartholomew's flesh hand. He can feel the hot liquid travel down his food pipe and hit his stomach. Later he imagines he can feel it buzzing neurons, hurrying his blood. People come and go as they sit. Some stop, as they did, at the desk, to exchange information with the person who sits behind it, while others move confidently through the waiting chamber, nodding or waving briefly as they pass beyond.

A male person seated behind a desk appears on the television screen and looks out so earnestly, speaks so directly that Bartholomew almost believes the person sees him. From a sheaf of papers on the desk before him, the man reads stories, one after another, and his stories are uniformly short, alike in lacking shape and resolution. Bartholomew listens closely, hoping to intuit some pattern or guiding principle behind the sequence of the stories, the juxtaposition of war and basketball and small ones building statues out of snow, but finds none that makes sense to him. As the person speaks, the waiting room fills with traffic, a purposeful and one-directional traffic, leaving. A new person arrives to replace the red-lipped female who, before he leaves, says to them, "Time to eat. There's no point in waiting now. The station manager's already gone to lunch."

The relief person sits behind the desk, draws something from a bag and begins to study it—a three-dimensional rectangle, mostly yellow, with a picture of a lurid red flower on it and, in black, some of the calligraphs that Brother Alice calls letters. The person divides the rectangle in two along a common side, and Bartholomew sees that there are papers bound inside. For what seems to be a fixed interval, the person stares at one paper, then turns to the next, over and over again.

"I'm hungry," Ringer whispers.

Ringer invokes Bartholomew's own hunger, a condition present but until now unacknowledged, and he can feel the emptiness of his stomach, walls of muscle reaching out for food and encountering only each other. Their last meal, especially prepared for them by Louis, was taken even before daylight came. "I'm hungry, too."

"We could try to find food," Ringer says, but his voice lacks enthusiasm.

Finding food will not be easy. There is money in their pockets, put there by Brother Alice, but they are unsure how to use it. They understand, from being told, that people outside go to special eating places to get their food, and that these can be found by looking through windows to see if the people inside are eating. "What is the special, please? What is your soup?" are questions Brother Alice tells them will almost always produce food, in spite of the inscrutability of the letter signs that fill the outside world. Still, even armed with the phrases "Excuse me, I don't read English well" and "How much does it cost?" the venture seems fraught with danger, the possibilities for error abundant.

"We could," Bartholomew says, keeping his own voice uncommitted.

"Or we could wait until the leader sees our tapes," Ringer suggests. "If he sees our tapes, he'll understand our problem in getting food. He could help us."

With relief, Bartholomew accepts this logic. The person behind the desk is too absorbed in his study to pay attention to them. Their hunger makes them silent. To sublimate, they watch the television screen, they listen.

Form, content, technique. Bartholomew studies them all, though the last is easiest to understand and the only to admire. The programs themselves are uniform in length, tediously so, whether their message is great or mundane, and interrupted at predictable intervals by a series of brief playlets exhorting people to buy things, most often compounds for the washing of clothes or floors or dishes, or for the relief of illness. Each person outside, it seems, is responsible for his own habitation, for his own pain.

The programs neither celebrate nor document. Perhaps if he understood the idiom of the outside better, he would understand too why the people on the sound track laugh. Boom, giggle, snort, trill, components of symphonic laughter. What is so funny?

The workers return, their one-way bustle fills the waiting room and passes; the whole building, while quiet, is less silent than when they were gone. On the television, games are replaced by plays. The dramas confuse Bartholomew, the tragedies—there are several, played back to back—fail to incite his pity. How do the people bear such surfeit of sadness? At the Place, the pain of art is respected, is measured, it is used sparingly and then to purpose. Sadness relieves sadness, it stretches the spirit. Here, on television, so many die that death grows meaningless.

"Their editing is very good," Ringer says. "Their sound is clear. There are more layers, more levels to their sound than to ours. Can you hear them?"

Bartholomew nods, then listens. His ears are not so fine as Ringer's, lack his sophistication, but instructed can hear a certain richness, a simultaneity of sounds impossible to achieve on the equipment at the Place. He hears Ringer's sigh of envy and understands his hunger for the machines that can produce such sound.

"You guys are sure persistent," the red-lipped receptionist says. "You must want to see the old man pretty bad. More coffee?"

More coffee. On the screen, a flat red cross grows three dimensional, begins to spin in deep tree-green space, revealing all its planar facets, dispelling as it does so the illusion of being an illusion.

"Look at that," Ringer breathes.

Bartholomew looks but would rather touch. Knows he cannot. The three-dimensional figure exists beyond the slightly convex surface of the screen. But behind the screen, inside the set are only tubes and mirrors, an eloquent vacuum, no room for dancing crosses, no deep green space. The coffee sings along his nerves, and Bartholomew imagines his red heart dancing in the green space of his chest. Brother Alice, too, is a song his nerves sing, a silver song, bells faintly echoing, and the low moan of a horn. Bartholomew does not need to say, not even to himself, I miss Brother Alice, I lean toward him, to know that this is true.

Bells and horns.

The red cross becomes a red star and the red star turns green, turns purple then yellow then finally white as it recedes, shrinking in recession until it is only a small white point in the upper right-hand corner of the screen, a fleck the green space swallows.

Winter darkness presses against the windows and there is an exodus of workers. The person at the desk turns off his machines and gathers his belongings. "Five o'clock." The clock face on the wall confirms it. Five oh two. At six the People will go to the dining hall to eat together. The man on the television reads once again the pointless anecdotes called news. Bartholomew's hunger pinches his stomach and his flippers are numb from the weight of the tapes. Beside him, Ringer rubs his eyes with his flesh hand.

"Good night now," the red-lipped female says.

36

THE OPERATOR IS A YOUNG MAN, his voice seductive. "Person-to-person call for Dr. Halliburton from Dr. Kleig." Alice identifies herself as Dr. Halliburton.

"Your party is on the line," the operator says. "Go ahead."

Kleig's voice is immediate, hearty. "Alice. Sorry about your job. I really am. On the other hand, it could be the best thing that ever happened to you."

"Are you calling to gloat?"

"Actually, I wanted the name of your tailor." He laughs. "Little joke. The truth is, I'm not planning to pursue my work in drag. You'll be pleased to know I've persuaded Harris that the Team owes it to you to help you find another job, despite your unorthodox departure."

"That was kind of you."

"You sound bitter, Alice. It doesn't suit you. Harris was very angry. I calmed him down."

She fails to offer the thanks he seems to expect and he goes on. "What I called about is this. I know Harris told you to get out on the thirty-first. That was when he was still mad. I've succeeded in convincing him how much your presence could help to ease the transition there. The People trust you." He pauses, then says, "It would make things easier for me, too, frankly. Stay a week or two. Brief me."

"Before the Team debriefs me."

"That's not my department, Alice. But I hope you'll stay awhile. I could use your help, and helping me could help to put you back in Briggs's good graces. Besides,

I'd like to see you again. I think we know we're compatible in some ways, if not in others."

"Are you authorized to speak for Harris Briggs?"

"All but the very last part. That's none of his business."

"I see."

"Will you stay?"

She counts the beats of her pause, not wanting to seem eager, then sighs a sigh loud enough to be heard long-distance. "I'll stay."

"Good girl. Expect us on the first, then."

"Who's coming? I mean, how many extra places should we set for dinner?"

"Oh, a dozen should do it. I'm bringing my medical staff, a few technicians, and a small security team. Though I'm sure the latter won't find too much to do."

"The threat is felt."

"I told Harris you weren't the type to do anything stupid. I'll see you in a few days, then."

"I'll be ready," Alice says. "Good-bye."

37

"ARE YOU TWO STILL HERE?"

After so much waiting, nothing retains the power to startle, but the voice captures their attention, it calls them forth. The question it asks seems to require no answer. They are demonstrably here.

"I saw you here at lunchtime," the voice says. It issues from a round face brown as Leda's was, from a head ridged with hair like garden rows, stripes of earth-brown scalp fallow between black rows. A broad mouth, brown-pink, smiles at them. As though they were nestlings, Bartholomew thinks, inadvertently amusing.

"We're waiting to see the station manager," Bartholomew says.

"Long gone. Without his Canadian Club by five oh five, the man disintegrates." He steps back from them, a zoom out to lengthen the shot, then says, "What are you selling, anyway?"

"Selling?"

"Come on."

"Come where?"

The person claps his two like hands, swings back identical brown arms. "Let's take it from the top. Are you guys for real?"

"We're makers of television," Ringer says.

"Job hunting?"

The person laughs, and even though the laughter is aimed at them, derisive, a substratum of good humor dulls offense. Bartholomew finds himself cheered. Apart from the taped laughter of the television, this is the first sound of mirth he's heard outside the Place.

"We have our work," Ringer replies. "We wanted to show him our tapes."

"Independents. I get it." When he shakes his head, bright beads dance and clatter at the ends of his braids. "Hey, I'm free-lance myself. I shoot, I run sound. Right now they've got me editing. But it's a bitch. This town's got more video freaks than plumbers. And most of them can't shoot for shit."

This outpouring of speech stuns Bartholomew. That it's friendly, he can tell, senses its authenticity, but strange words punch holes in the flow, holes he falls through in pursuit of sense. By the time he surfaces, meaning has outdistanced him. He stares, and Ringer too is silent.

The person stares back. "You've got a way with words, huh? Okay, I'll keep it simple. How come you want to show the man your tapes?"

Ringer looks at Bartholomew, Bartholomew looks back. The question hangs between them, and neither is certain of the answer. There is no answer, only guesses. Bartholomew widens his eyes, interrogative, Ringer nods slightly and the cut is made. "If we tell you," Bartholomew says, "then you must help us. That is the code. Are you willing to accept our code?"

"Sweet Jesus, you guys are weird." Head shakes, beads tumble. Pink-brown, the grin widens to show broad white teeth. What the hell. How often do you. "I read Dumas myself, even though he's a honkey. Okay. You got it." Brown hand, pink-nailed, clasps Bartholomew's flesh hand, grabs Ringer's. "The Three Mouseketeers. Honor. Duty. All that stuff. My name is Michel Boucicault. What's yours?"

38

Starsky and Hutch, in late-night rerun, crouch behind a concrete bulkhead, their weapons held ready. "Those are guns," Alice tells Boris.

"What are they for?" he asks.

The question is soon answered. The heroes aim and shoot. The loud report startles Boris. Several characters, male, presumably evil, are hit, fall, die. At the sight of blood, Boris averts his face.

"It isn't real," Alice reminds him. "No one is really hurt."

When Boris looks up again, the dead are gone. Starsky and Hutch give chase in a car. "I've dreamed of machines like those," Boris says. "How do they run?"

"They have internal-combustion engines. They run on gasoline. But back to guns. The Fathers will have them when they come. That gives them the power to take our lives."

"Do we have guns?"

"No," she tells him. "It's wrong to use guns."

"Why is the same thing right for them and wrong for us?"

"I haven't got time for a lesson in ethics," Alice says. "Accept it, Boris. What we need is to find a way to take away their guns and gain power over them without anyone, them or us, getting hurt."

Boris thinks a moment, then says, "We'll have to surprise them, then. Do they all have two arms and two legs?"

"They do."

"That makes it difficult. But I have an idea," Boris says.

"Good. I hoped you would. You'll have all the help and all the materials you need. You have to work fast."

"I will," Boris promises. His gaze reverts to the television screen. The chase continues. An old Impala convertible screeches around a tight corner, rear end rocking, with a black and white police car close on its tail pipes. "I will work fast," Boris says. "But before I start, could I study these machines a little longer, please?"

39

COUNTING, still unfamiliar, comes slow. Sixteen. A matrix four by four of monitors embedded in the wall. The faces of the screens are blank, black. Already Ringer approaches the console, a tilted table surface wide as the room itself, banked with buttons, levers, dials. His eyes, exploring, caress the machine, his flesh hand reaches out, reverent and wanting, to touch this knob, that stick. Below the console, on either side, patch panels bristle with cabled connections and beyond the control room itself, on the other side of a tinted-glass half-wall, Bartholomew recognizes the news set, the desk where the announcer sat to read his stories, the background wall clock, even the stories themselves, disarrayed now. Three cameras larger than Bartholomew has ever seen or imagined, cameras tall as people and mounted each on three splayed, wheeled feet stare blindly at the newsreader's vacant chair. Lights bigger than the cameras arc above the set, dark now.

"Hardware junkies." Michel smiles at their wonder. "This is Studio B. A's bigger, but they're using it."

"Do you work here always?" Ringer asks.

"No. Hell no. I'm free-lance, like I said. Right now they've got me editing tape of this charity auction ball. Fat ladies dancing, bald guys in tuxedoes." Palm perpendicular to the floor, he shakes his hand in air. "Boring. I produce my own stuff over at Sunshine Studios. When I've got a job that pays the rent."

"At the Place," Ringer says, "we have only two cameras. Small cameras. Small enough to carry."

"Portapaks," Michel says. "Nothing wrong with that.

You got a good eye and a steady hand, you're all set. Let's have a look at these tapes."

He reaches for Brother Alice's briefcase and Bartholomew surrenders it to him. His lap feels naked without its weight, and cold. Michel clicks open the latches of the case and lifts the lid. Six videotapes nestle in three neat rows.

One by one, Michel uncases the tapes and feeds them into heads until all six are placed, ready to play. "Now we'll see what kind of bullshit you guys've been feeding me." Pushes six buttons. In the center of the matrix a six-screen rectangle lights up, three squares by two, six still-frame images invoke the Place. The gardens. Beatrice the mime. Lucas's heart awash in Lucas blue. The nestling Hanford. A wide shot of the dining hall, the People eating. A goose in flight.

Michel's sharp inhalation becomes a whistle, leaving. Bartholomew sees his smile, habitual, is shocked away, his eyes wide as he reads images, left to right, up down, reads them again. The lost smile transmigrates to Bartholomew as he sees his home, his People on the screens. Ringer looks anxious, and Bartholomew can feel how much he wants Michel's approval, the acknowledgment of a colleague.

"Here goes."

The circuits close, the pictures move, the booth fills up with sound.

I am Beatrice the mime . . . *voice of the People* . . . *here we eat* . . . music in flight, its beat synchronous with the beating of the wings of goose. *Nestling.*

The goose becomes Leda. Beatrice becomes Clotho. The camera zooms in on Lucas's mouth. One nestling replaces another and Bartholomew's eyes seek out the bottom left square, nest there, waiting, until Brother Alice in his silver suit appears and Bartholomew welcomes the image, receives it with his whole body, a drop of moisture and a surge of blood, his heartbeat audible inside his ears.

"Holy shit."

Michel drops into the swivel chair, he walks it closer to the screens, then turns away, leans back so that the chair springs creak. He shakes his head in arcs of small circumference, a gesture meant not to communicate but to dispel. He looks back to the matrix, where the tapes play on, his eyes move over the screens and then encompass them. Stab, jab, his fingers press buttons. The pictures freeze, sound stops.

Into the silence, Ringer says, "Our studio is small. Our equipment is nothing compared to this. The toys of small ones."

"I don't believe it."

"Our sound is very simple. Our lights are small."

"Absolutely unreal."

"Only the two of us, Bartholomew and I, know how to make television at all," Ringer says.

"I feel like I've seen it all before. I've seen it in my dreams. Only I called them nightmares."

"We didn't have much time to make the census. It's repetitive. The shots are dull. Just documentary."

"It's going to blow them away."

"If we could use your cameras"—Ringer gestures toward the empty studio—"we could do much better."

Michel spins his chair toward them. "It's beautiful. It's the most beautiful damn stuff I've ever seen." His fingers slide into the fallow rows between his braids and crown his skull. Bartholomew has studied his face long enough by now to recognize the exaltation on it.

"We could do better," Ringer says.

Michel's brown eyes with their black centers fix on

Bartholomew's eyes and the question is fierce in his look.

"It's true, isn't it? That story you told me. No special effects. Hell, you couldn't fake that stuff. Not even Speilberg. Not with a billion dollars. It's the real thing."

Bartholomew nods. From the left-hand screen on the bottom of the second row, from a face exquisitely silver, Brother Alice's eyes, blue and green, look back at him.

40

ALICE WAITS beside the phone. All day she has waited, never venturing beyond the circle of its summons. They have the right coins, they have the right numbers in their proper sequence, and she prepared them for either contingency, punch or dial, but the phone does not ring. Black plastic and inscrutable, it sits on her desk, indifferent to questions, until her anxiety turns to hostility, and she begins to hate the telephone.

Several hours ago, she copied the number of the television station out of the book. At two o'clock, she told herself she would call at three if she had not heard from them. At three o'clock, she told herself she would call at four; at four, she decided to wait until four-thirty. It is now four forty-nine, and Alice is sure they both are dead. She tries to imagine that they are well but occupied, whole but irresponsible, but her imagination fails her. At four fifty-three, she would rather know than wonder. Twice, Alice rehearses the numbers that will access them, then picks up the receiver.

There is no dial tone. There is no hum, no static, no resonance at all. Thank you, Dr. Kleig. Mother Bell's umbilicus is cut and tied. Bartholomew is born into the world.

41

BY THE TIME they reach Michel's dwelling, three rooms he calls an apartment, Bartholomew is exhausted.

They were careful in the restaurant, he and Ringer, as they tried, suppressing wonder, to emulate Michel's oblivious ease. The food was filling but tasted strange. His wheelchair would not fit through the doors of the bus. To Michel's dwelling the journey, walk and wheel, was long and the paths too narrow for three to move abreast. Without time to explore or to ponder them, the many objects and events they passed remained unintelligible. A small, four-legged animal, its coat shaggy as Ringer's beneath his clothes and lighter brown, sniffed at his wheels, then baring pointed teeth, pursued him, crying a hoarse and hostile cry.

The walls of Michel's apartment are covered with shiny unframed pictures—of outside people singing or dancing or simply staring at the camera, of strange animals, of geometric patterns and unpeopled landscapes improbable as dreams. His rooms are full of smells Bartholomew has never smelled before.

Sometimes, at the intersection of car and foot paths, they found inclines to accommodate his chair, but as they approached Michel's dwelling, the paths grew narrower, were less well-lit and abutted the car paths with sharp low stairs Michel called curbs. Michel and Ringer lifted his chair then, down, across the car-ways, up.

"Make yourselves at home," Michel says, and Ringer settles on one end of a long, low chair.

People stared at him, he could feel it, but when he raised his eyes, averted theirs, so that their faces resembled masks, resembled Beatrice's mime face in instants of repose. So many faces, regular, similar, repetitive, so many symmetrically paired eyes full of denial that Bartholomew came to believe the people outside shared only one face, one hard and unresponsive look.

Michel brings them red juice in clear glasses. It smells of chemicals and must and tastes like fire.

At the entrance to Michel's dwelling place, stairs. They sat him on the lowest step while Michel carried his chair up the stairs outside, up the stairs inside to his rooms. Then Michel and Ringer made a provisional seat of their joined hands, slid him onto it and carried him, as nestlings or the limbless are sometimes carried at the Place. They carried him gently and without complaint but Bartholomew, used to the autonomy of ramp and derrick, felt the touch of their hands as an intrusion, a condescension of flesh that made his skin grow hot and wet with shame.

Michel places a black disc on the spindle of a strange machine and when he presses a button the machine's arm moves itself to the outer circumference of the circle. On its flat axis, the disc begins to rotate. Soon music fills the rooms.

Bartholomew has never felt this way before, this way he feels with his whole body, with his being, feelings physical and metaphorical synced and stymied, his senses so hard exercised they lock in tetanus, a state of excitation so intense and so sustained it resembles numbness, as if the peaks and valleys of the Excitement had been leveled into a single, insupportable sensation. The music pleases and repels him. He is fleetingly grateful that Brother Alice is not here, to know him in this state.

The beat of the music is merciless, a fast forced march against a simple melody. A singer chants a single phrase over and over, varying only the loudness, the vociferousness of his incantation. Sometimes the voice is soft, almost tender, sometimes seems mocking, most often angry, now and then sounds truly mad. Above the instruments, Bartholomew can sometimes hear the hard rasp of the singer's breathing.

Michel seems captive of the music. His eyes are closed, his boot pounds out the rhythm, his beaded braids keep double time. Now and then his lips appear to mouth the words the singer sings. Ringer leans forward into the music and his whole body looks alert. The song ends with a clash of drums, and after a second's pause another starts to play, the same beat retarded to a tempo of lament, as a heart slows after exercise. Bartholomew relaxes a little but is not released. Ringer's flesh hand marks time on his knee. The machine's arm reads the disc in smaller and smaller circles until the music ends.

Michel gets up. "That's it. I want to cut your tapes to those songs."

"But our tapes are for the television station," Bartholomew says. "We have to persuade the station manager to show them."

"He'll never do it. Never. You show that jerk your tapes and he'll be on the hotline to the FBI. Your story gets killed and you end up in jail."

"Brother Alice told us that might happen," Ringer says. "We came prepared to take that chance."

"No chance," Michel says. "It's a sure thing. I don't know who this Brother Alice is exactly, but he must be pretty naïve. Besides, the man's some kind of war hero from Korea. He's so red, right and blue he wouldn't mess with the feds to save his grandma. But," he says, "fate smiled. That's why you met this Haitian black boy. That's why some little voice in me said, hey, check out those two freaky-looking guys, why not? We're going to help each other. You help me, and I help you."

"How can we help you?" Ringer asks.

"By letting me help you. Let me cut those tapes to Starfish. Let me show them. It'll be the best damn video anybody's ever done."

Bartholomew's mind feels as jammed as his senses. "I don't understand," he says.

Michel's excitement makes him pace. "It's what I do. Charity balls for Channel Five's just a sideline. I'm a video artist, my friends. One of the best in town. The best, after this comes down." He opens his hands to them, instructing and imploring. "Those tapes of yours, see. That's what everybody's been trying to do. Getting stoned out and trying to peek into the future. How's it going to be for us? Mushroom clouds and zombies. Well, this is it. This is how it's going to be. And you and me and Starfish are going to show them."

"Who is Starfish?" Ringer asks. "Will he help us?"

Michel laughs. "It's not a he, it's a group. A band. Seven of them, not counting tech. Hot. Starfish is number three on the charts now, that song you heard. It's going platinum. And we," he says, "are going to make the video."

"The Place is in danger," Bartholomew says. "We haven't got much time. Our only hope is to get our message to the people."

"We'll get it there. Is Saturday soon enough for you?"

"When is Saturday?"

"Four days." Michel looks at the clock strapped to his wrist. "No, three. It's after midnight. There's a sold-out concert at the Dome, and Starfish headlines. Twenty thousand people are going to see those tapes. The media will be there." Michel paces away with syncopated steps and returns with a large bottle full of the dark red juice. "More?" He fills their empty glasses. "Drink up. I'm going to phone Jim Steward. He's Starfish's manager."

Michel goes to another room to make his call. For the first time in hours, Ringer and Bartholomew are alone together. Meeting, their eyes are full of questions. At last Ringer asks, "Is this the right thing for the Place?"

Bartholomew wishes the question were Brother Alice's, not his, to answer. For a moment, he tries to clear his mind, through force of intellect to access Brother Alice's wisdom, but the circuit is imaginary and will not close. With only his own experience to guide him, his reason untested against such complexity, his intuition no more acute than any small one's, the question seems impossible to answer. And the answer is inevitable. They have met Michel. Michel is willing to help them. This is what happened, not something else.

Bartholomew looks at Ringer and slowly nods his head. "Yes, it must be," he says.

42

"CLOTHO IS RIGHT," Boris says. "Capture their senses first, and their bodies will be easier to seize."

The round pillow that supports Clotho's chin above his cart tends to enforce a somewhat grim expression but now he smiles, pleased by the inventor's approbation. "Art enhances all things," he says.

Alice, in turn, is pleased by the success of the collaboration. Working with Boris and Clotho has not always been easy. Both are temperamental, Boris made so by intelligence, Clotho because he is extraordinarily, almost morbidly sensitive. She has sometimes been less than patient herself, irritable or dismissive. With her disguise, she's put off a portion of her detachment. Having laid aside her claim of a hotline to the gods, her ideas are simply ideas, no weightier than theirs and no more deserving of execution. They have learned to disagree, and she values their contention even though it sometimes wearies her.

She's tired now, body and brain. Only duty keeps her eyelids raised. Her watch says 1 A.M. and Alice smiles at her comrades. "We've gotten a lot done tonight. I think we can afford to stop. There's an hour left before the couriers come, and I'd like to rest." She sighs, looking at Clotho. "Would you like me to help you with your derrick? Your neighbors all will be asleep by now."

"I can help him," Boris says. "His house is next to mine and I'm still awake."

"I accept your help," Clotho says. "At least until you invent a derrick for the limbless that requires no help. I, too, am tired."

Alice makes the effort to rise and walks with them to

the door of her living quarters. As they move down the hallway, a snatch of their conversation carries back to her, Boris saying, "It would require some kind of sensor, so the derrick could position itself."

The door closes on her solitude. Alice takes off her shoes and stretches out on the sofa, only to find that now she has the time to rest, she is no longer able. Bartholomew's face flickers on the backs of her closed lids. From sign-on to sign-off, shifts of the People have monitored the broadcast waves but have seen nothing to suggest the mission is completed. On the other hand, nothing to confirm its failure, no "Mysterious Mutants Found Dead," no "Police Today Arrested . . ." If, then. Either/or. Behind one set of anxieties, another lies in wait.

Alice gets up. She would not mind thinking if thinking were productive, but her circuits seem stuck in a futile loop, the same thoughts in the same form cycling. Her daybook lies open on the desk and she bends over it to count the days again. Two left until K-Day, she calls it that, the day that Kleig arrives, the day she makes her changed allegiance known. If the plan works, it will buy Bartholomew and Ringer more time. How much? A few days, two or five. Alice leafs through the pages of her calendar, time past and coming, squares on paper, numbers, moving quickly through her moving fingers.

A new thought breaks the loop and stops her rifling. Time has another meaning. She turns back to November and finds it mid-month—the female hieroglyph, inverted two-armed cross stuck to a circle she's used for years to note the onset of menstruation. Sunday to Sunday she counts weeks and finds them six. Too many. She counts again, breathes deeply. Closes her eyes and questions her body. Why have you forgotten? Her stomach gurgles slightly, her ears pop as she listens.

Alice cups her right breast in her left hand, she tries to remember. The dates of the convocation are marked on her calendar, but Kleig used a condom. Used several. They had a fancy name and an exotic scent. Not Kleig. Thank god, not Kleig. Perhaps the menopause. It would be early, but she's lived hard, lived strange. Or stress. There's been a lot of that. Perhaps even now it's starting, begun its descent. What was it someone called it? The tears of an unfertilized ovum. She wills her cervix to cramp, to make the reassuring pain.

Or.

Alice laughs. If not Kleig. It is funny. Is it possible? Nature's little joke, her irony. Natural humor. Is she the victim or the perpetrator? It is very funny. And if it's true, there's not a damn thing she can do about it. She looks at the calendar again. Too few squares for a quick trip to a chic clinic, discreet and antiseptic.

It's in Nature's hands, Nature the great abortionist, reputed to hate freaks and punish mating infractions with infertility. If it's true, what is it? It *is* funny. She slaps her knee, laughing.

Alice doubles over, touches chin to knee and laughs. *I am the crucible.* She laughs until she cries.

43

THE IMAGES ARE LOOPED, the loop repeats: Lucas, Clotho, Peter, Hanford, Joseph, Beatrice, Louis, Boris, Ringer, Brother Alice, Lucas again. The images move fast and regular as heartbeats, their tenure on the screen is no longer than the journey of a shooting star across the winter sky. The music is the genius of the tape. Its rhythm dictates the visual rhythm, the dizzying speed at which the images pass by. As a clock ticks, that reliably, Ringer's flesh hand taps the console.

"That's it. Do it," Michel says, and Ringer's steel fingers press the button.

"God, you're good," Michel tells Ringer. "I never saw anybody cut to music the way you do."

Bartholomew watches the slow bright dawn of Ringer's smile. There was a time his own praise could incite that smile, part vanity, part pure delight in craft, on Ringer's face. It seems a long time ago, now, that they were master and apprentice. Now Ringer indentures himself to Michel, he leans toward his knowledge and flowers at his praise while Bartholomew looks on.

"Now watch this," Michel says. He pushes buttons on the console and begins the loop again. This time the People are transformed, their outlines thick and luminous, their mass, inside the darker outlines, pale washes of pure color. Their features are abstracted to gouges of luminous shadow. Painterly, Bartholomew thinks; Clotho might see and render them like that. Well, yes and no. He might conceive the effect, he might execute it as well, but never so uniformly as the machine. Never in motion. As he watches, Bartholomew thinks of a dozen, a hundred of his own tapes that might be enriched by the effect. The colors seem to pulsate as the figures move. Michel slows the tape and the frantic action of the images becomes a stately dance to music that sounds drugged. Smears of color bleed off the images, the screen retains the memory of past motion even as the figures move presently.

"It's beautiful," Ringer says, and Bartholomew says, "Yes." Michel looks up from the console to grin at them, and for a moment all three are peers, bound by their love for the making of television, and for the tools of television.

Michel freezes the tape. "So far, so good," he says. "Now comes the solo. I haven't figured out the cut."

Ringer turns to look at his old master. "Bartholomew juxtaposes images very well," he says.

Bartholomew feels himself blush. Michel laughs. "The way you guys talk," he says. Then: "Come on, Bartholomew. Do us a little juxta-whosis."

Bartholomew wheels his chair toward the console and for a moment studies the posterized image still frozen on the monitor. It happens to be Brother Alice speaking, his scales purpled by special effects, the pattern of his overlapping scales outlined in purple/black, his mouth a darkly purple luminous mass, a purple cave. Bartholomew releases his senses, his eyes travel deep into the darkest reaches of the purple, spelunking, while another part of his mind reviews the other tapes, the images available for use.

"There is a flower," he says. "About that size, about that place. I shot it at the start of the third season, when the gardens are in bloom. There is a sequence of flowers. There are flowers on the table when Ringer comes of age. There is a close-up of Brother Alice giving Ringer his work. His mouth is red. He speaks. As he speaks, his mouth can become a flower again." He pauses. "I think it can."

"It can," Michel says. He pats the switcher. "Any miracle you want, my friend."

"And the flowers can become the faces of the nestlings," Bartholomew says. "Or of the People, greeting the nestlings."

"I like it," Michel says. "As long as it times out to the interlude."

"It will," Ringer says. "We can make it match."

Hours later, it does. Fragmentary images make a new mosaic, cemented by the sweet/sad glue of an alto saxophone. It is no longer documentary, the flow of images no longer represents accurately how things transpire at the Place or how long they take to happen, but the new thing they've made seems valid to Bartholomew nonetheless, emotionally if not historically so. Their tape evokes the Place so well it makes him deeply homesick. The tenderness of the People as they welcome the nestlings is not lost, their elation as Ringer reveals his prostheses and receives his work is evident. The magic of the machines has not stolen but intensified the magic of the rituals. The new syntax of editing he's learned—the wipes, color keys, insets, the split-screen images—have increased his eloquence and extended the power of his language. Bartholomew's heart speaks images, and he is pleased with his speech.

Michel regards the final still-frame of the sequence, a close-up so extreme it erases context and makes an object of Brother Alice's green omniscient eye, then gets up from his swivel chair and stretches his arms toward the ceiling. "Some place," he says. "I'd kind of like to see it for myself someday." He flexes work-stiff fingers, then uses them to rub his tired eyes. "If Starfish doesn't love this tape, they're idiots."

Bartholomew is pleased enough by the tape to need no further praise, but he can see that Ringer is not yet satisfied. He wheels himself close enough to his friend to put his flesh hand on Ringer's shoulder. "What do you think?" he asks.

Instead of answering, Ringer turns to Michel. "What do *you* think? Do you think that I, that we are good enough to be makers of television outside the Place?"

Michel looks at each of them in turn, his pink/brown smile benevolent. "You looking for a job?" he says. "No question. I'd hire you guys in a minute."

Turning, Bartholomew sees pride in Ringer's eyes.

44

AT THE SIGHT OF HER, Kleig's smile freezes into a
parody of smiling, his eyes look hurt by surprise. Behind
him, his team is silent and unmoving. They stare at her.
Even the two men most closely flanking Kleig, the ones
she takes to be security because their faces and their
bodies look harder than the rest, are temporarily arrested by the splendor, by the iconographic power of
Brother Alice. Kleig was wrong to discount the magic of
her silver suit, and pays for it now. She, magnificently,
safely silver, wins the advantage; the tone of the encounter is hers to set. Without speaking, she inclines
her silver head to them; a sweep of her silver arm invites them to enter and cautions them to enter quietly,
and with respect.

Kleig tries to laugh, but his laughter is aborted by the
silver finger she places to her lips, by the silence she lets
grow after the door clicks shut behind them. Alice motions them to stay where they are—eight men and
three women, by a hasty count—while she walks slowly
up the corridor to the place where Lucas waits. Their
responses to seeing him are audible and staggered, like
the explosions of a string of firecrackers. One of the
women, she notices, is very young, too young and
pretty to be useful, except for recreation. Alice nods to
Lucas, and he speaks, his great voice never larger or
more commanding. "My name is Lucas. I speak for the
People. In their name, I bid you welcome to the Place."

Paralyzed by wonder, Kleig and his team make easy
prey. Swiftly, silently, the net drops down on them, a
fine, dense mesh, and Boris, his prosthetic hand con-
verted to a pulley, tightens the rope until the net is

closed around them. Some of the captives fall. Their tongues are loosened; they curse and shout. One of the women screams. Peter, Louis and Adolph emerge from Alice's quarters with the syringes and she joins them at their task, plunging the needles without ceremony into legs or arms or buttocks, whatever comes to hand, turning the squirming bundle so that none escapes injection. Alice turns out the lights, to confuse them, to hasten sleep.

A voice, unmistakably Kleig's, speaks in the darkness: "Goddamn it, Alice, you won't get by with this," and she responds with a smile invisible to him. "Can't reach my gun," another voice laments. Gradually the sounds of struggle diminish. Alice smells ammonia in the darkness, urine. When it has been quiet for a long time, Alice turns on the light. Boris approaches the net and kicks at the captives. No one cries out. Nothing moves. Boris releases the rope and they pull the net away. The bodies of the captives are limp and loose, their faces slack with sleep.

One by one, they drag bodies from the pile, one by one search them for weapons. The security men wear holstered revolvers. Loose in Kleig's sport-coat pocket, Alice finds a snub-nosed handgun, cheap and mean. The others are unarmed. After the frisking, the captives are bound hand and foot, derricked onto carts or into wheelchairs and rolled away to separate, guarded rooms throughout the dwelling houses.

As Kleig is being strapped into a wheelchair, his eyes roll open, wholly white at first, until his pupils descend, until his lenses admit the image of Brother Alice, silver face and high green eye. He tries to speak but his tongue is too heavy, his larynx too languid to make words. Alice sticks a needle in his thigh and presses down the plunger. The drug insists on sleep. His head rolls forward, chin to chest. When all eleven outsiders have been dealt with, the great bell rings for a long time to let the People know the battle has been won.

All afternoon, via intercom, Alice receives reports of their awaking. Kleig, double-dosed, sleeps on. One of the women captives will not stop crying. After several hours, Peter, who guards her, who has done his best to comfort her, is close to tears himself. "She won't eat or drink," he tells Alice. "I can't get near her."

Alice enters the room as Alice, ordinary and unsilver. The woman's face is turned toward the wall, but Alice can tell by the tangle of long hair on her pillow it is the young woman, Kleig's special pet. She says nothing, only waits for curiosity to do its work. At last the girl turns to look at her, and Alice sees her prettiness is defaced by crying, her eyes pink and puffy, her pale cheeks slashed with red.

"There's nothing to be afraid of," Alice says. "The People are good. No one will hurt you."

"Oh god," the girl murmurs, and her shoulders lift in a dry sob.

"I'm Alice Halliburton. What's your name?"

The girl gives it grudgingly. Her name is Laurie.

"Didn't Kleig warn you the honeymoon might not be easy?"

"He had a gun. He showed it to me. He said he'd . . ." She looks at Alice, eyes widening. "You're Brother Alice?"

Alice nods. "He said he'd kill me."

The girl shakes her head, as if expelling nightmares. "He didn't tell me they'd be so strange, or so ugly. I can't even look at them."

"You'll get used to it."

"Are you going to kill me?"

"Of course not. We'll take good care of you, and when the time comes, we'll let you go."

A provisional hopefulness elevates the girl's eyebrows. "Couldn't you put me someplace where I wouldn't have to see them?"

"I could but I won't," Alice tells her. "I want you to get to know the People."

The girl's answer is unthinking and sincere. "I'd rather die," she says.

Her petulance makes Alice angry, and for a brief moment, she lets anger rule her body. She slaps the girl. Slaps her again with words. "If there's another war, your children are going to look like the People. If you live long enough to have them. You'd best get used to it."

The girl's whimper gives way to a flat reflective tone. Not looking at Alice, she says, "He told me it was a laboratory technician's job. I was supposed to work in his lab."

Her helplessness drains Alice of her fury; it breaks, recedes. The undertow sucks away precious energy. "The world is a laboratory," she says wearily. "It has been for a long time. We're all expendable."

The girl is only another victim, Alice sees that. She sees her youth without jealousy now, and pities her. Seats herself on the edge of the bed, touches the limp hair tangled on the girl's forehead, finally helps her unresistingly to sit and hugs her, an embrace that demands forgiveness and insists on commonality. "I'm sorry," Alice says. "I didn't want to hurt you." She lays the girl back on her pillow.

"Kleig says you're crazy," the girl tells her.

Unable to refute the allegation, Alice only shrugs. "Let Peter help you. He's kind and gentle." Rising, she smiles. "Don't worry, Laurie," she says. "Everything is going to be all right."

45

THE PERSON CALLED JIM STEWARD, the person who is the manager of the band called Starfish claps his palm down on Michel's outstretched palm. The person called Jim Steward is two-armed, two-legged and symmetrical; his hair is very short, a bristled helmet; a gold star shines on the lobe of one of two identical ears; his clothes are cut of leather and make soft noises as he moves in them. Michel says he is an important person, more important than the manager of the television station. Michel says it is important that he like their tape.

Jim Steward looks at the clock on his wrist. "Let's make it quick," he says. "We've got a tech rehearsal at eight." His pale face wears an expression of cultivated impatience and his voice insists on his authority.

Michel seems willing to accept both. "Right," he says. "This won't take long. Sit down."

Jim Steward takes possession of the chair. Michel pulls a thin white stick from the pocket of his shirt and holds it up. "Smoke?"

Jim Steward nods, Michel puts the white stick between his lips and lights one end of it. He inhales deeply, then hands the stick to Jim Steward, who in turn inhales. "Run it," he says, and his words emerge enveloped in pale smoke.

Michel turns out the one dim light still burning and the control room grows wholly dark. Lucas appears, a blue light on the monitor, and music fills the room. The tape they've spent so many hours editing is only as long as the song. Six and one half minutes long. They know every note of the melody, every chord of every riff, each refinement of the sound mix, the beating of the drums. They know it backward as well as forward. The tape, audio and video, the marriage of the tracks, is unerasable in them.

Jim Steward watches silently. When the tape is over and the room quiet, he says, "Again." The white stick is small between his fingers, the control room filled with fragrant smoke. Michel rewinds the tape and plays it again.

"Enough," Jim Steward says, after the third viewing. Michel turns on the lights, all of the lights this time, though Jim Steward still faces the monitor and still does not see them, Bartholomew and Ringer, at the back of the room. "How much?" he asks Michel.

"How much is it worth to you?" Michel asks, and his smile extends to them, waiting against the wall.

"You know," Jim Steward says. "You know what you've got. You know I want it."

"Tell me," Michel says.

"So it's great. Fantastic. I don't know where it came from. You must be sick or crazy or both. But you did it. Raw tough ugly beauty. That's how it's going to be. That's what the kids saw when they looked. Okay? You want more crap about art, or do you want to make a deal?"

"I can't do business without my partners, man," Michel says. He points to the back of the room, reveals them. Seeing them, Jim Steward's mask falls for a moment and his face looks human. Human, he looks scared. "Bartholomew and Ringer," Michel says. "The tape is theirs. I helped them edit it. You might say," Michel says, "that I'm their business manager."

Jim Steward stares at them. Bartholomew says hello. Jim Steward looks to Michel. "Who are they?" he asks. "What are they?"

"Just like it says in the song, Jim," Michel tells him.

"They're the light at the end of the cyclotron tunnel. They're what happens after the end."

Jim Steward shakes his head and the star on his earlobe flashes gold. "What was in that joint?" he asks Michel.

"Reality," Michel says. He motions to them, *Come forward,* and they come. For a moment before they drop, Jim Steward's eyes meet Bartholomew's and his look is neutral as a lens, without opinion.

Michel laughs softly. "So, you want to hear the story, Jim?"

The person called Jim Steward rubs hard at his forehead with his fingertips, he looks at Bartholomew and Ringer through the vees of his spread digits. "Do I have a choice?" he says.

46

ON SO COLD A NIGHT, the voice of the great bell calls with special clarity; it is the ring of tiny hammers mining stars from darkness, the song the moon sings in her loneliness. It is a breaking. It calls the People and they fill the paths converging on the dining hall, the snow crust squealing under foot and wheel, their words, as they converge, rising in balloons of steam. The captives are brought from their rooms to join the mealtime procession. Disabled by their bonds, they come in wheelchairs and come silently. Inside the hall, which is warm and brightly lit and smells deliciously of food, the captives are wheeled to empty places, no two together, there to dine. As solicitously and as expertly as the limbless, they are fed.

"More meat, or peaches?" Peter asks, and for a moment it is hard for Laurie, so otherwise dependent, to remember she can speak. "Peaches, please," she says at last, and finds her words bring peaches, sweet and slippery on her tongue. While she eats, Peter feeds himself, and after a while, the alternation is rhythmic and efficient.

At first, she circumscribes her gaze, looks only at the food or at Peter, whom her eyes by now accept, but the voices around her, vital and various, are a temptation she can't resist. One at a time and guardedly, she dares to look at those nearby her, a female dwarf, a man without a nose or earflaps, a person of indeterminate sex plying silverware skillfully with a mechanical hand. Because visually she anticipates a certain pattern, she is shocked each time to find it violated in some new way; each time, some twinge of empathy requires that she imagine her own self similarly afflicted. The People, as she looks at them, look back. They smile or nod or even speak to her.

"I hope you enjoy your dinner," one says.

"I am," she replies.

"What is your work?" another asks.

"I'm a lab technician," she says. She doesn't know if these people know what a lab technician is, or if they nod and smile to be polite. The food is well-prepared and filling; eating half of it restores her hunger and eating the other half satisfies it. Exhaustion helps make the strange seem commonplace and she begins to accept the People as she accepts the aberrations of her dreams. Peter lifts her glass and she sucks apple juice through the straw. When she's done drinking, he wipes her lips dry with a napkin.

By now she is bold enough to turn her head, and doing so finds Kleig, two rings away and forty-five degrees to her left. She has never seen him angry but knows he is, from the thin line of his mouth under his moustache, inside his beard, and the hard glaze of his eyes. As she watches, a small-headed, big-shouldered man beside him lifts a forkful of meat and rice to Kleig's mouth. Kleig makes as if to accept it, then spits it out, shaking his head violently from side to side. A few grains of rice, a dribble or two of gravy cling to his beard.

From her vantage, Alice too sees Kleig's bad manners. It will take him quite a while to starve and the only damage he can do in the interim is to his own dignity. She feels a little guilty for her pleasure at the sight of him, helpless and graceless, his suavity debunked. But guilt is not compassion. Most of the captives, less rigid, suffer themselves to be fed. A few, looking as earnest and reluctant to offend as foreign exchange students, converse with the People around them, and these Alice takes to be the real scientists of the group, made flexible by innate curiosity. Only the security men, positioned out of one another's sight and Kleig's, affect an arrogance similar to his.

When the meal is done and the tables cleared, Alice signals Lucas to announce the evening's entertainment. "Ernestine has made a new play, and tonight we will see it for the first time. The play is called *War*. Lupe and Darwin are the players."

At the center of the hall, the round bare platform begins to rotate slowly. Lupe wheels his chair up the ramp and onto the stage. He flings his arms open wide and breathes deeply, tilts back his head and smiles upward at the warmth of the sun on his face. Bending forward, he picks an imaginary flower, inhales its perfume. Offstage, a whistle warbles a few sweet, patterned notes, repeats them, and Lupe cocks his head, listening to birds.

Darwin strides onstage, his feet loud on the ramp. A scowl distorts his face. Lupe nods at him. "Good morning, Darwin."

Darwin's grunt in response disavows the goodness of the morning.

"It's a beautiful day," Lupe says.

Darwin tramples the imaginary flowers. "It is not."

"The sun is out," Lupe says. "The birds are singing." He lifts his eyes to scan the horizon. "It's not every day the sky's so blue."

"The sky is not blue," Darwin says. "The sky is green."

Lupe looks surprised. He looks at the sky. He laughs.

"Why are you laughing?" Darwin asks.

"Because you made a joke. You said the sky is green."

"The sky *is* green," Darwin says.

"The sky is blue," Lupe says. "I've never seen it bluer."

Darwin's voice grows tight and rasping. "The sky is green."

Lupe looks down. "The grass is green." Looks up, around him. "The trees are green. The sky is blue."

Darwin slaps Lupe's face. "The sky is green."

Lupe touches his smarting cheek. He looks at Darwin with concern. "Are you ill, Darwin? Is that why you think the sky is green?"

Darwin's body stiffens. He clenches his fists, his chin thrusts forward as he speaks. "I'm not sick, I'm right. The sky is green."

"Look at the sky," Lupe cajoles. "How can you look at that sky and tell me it's green? Come on, look at it."

"I don't need to look. I know. The sky is green."

Lupe knows, too. "The sky," he says, "is blue."

In an instant, Darwin's arm draws tight around Lupe's throat. Darwin squeezes. "Say the sky is green." He tightens his hold, and a murmur of distress rises among the People. Suddenly, Darwin loosens his grip and Lupe's head droops forward. He coughs. "Say it," Darwin says. "Say the sky is green."

With a protective hand nursing his injured throat, Lupe whispers, "The sky is blue."

Darwin grabs Lupe's hair and jerks his head backward. He draws a gun, one of the guns seized earlier, from the pocket of his smock and holds it close to Lupe's temple. Only Alice, the captives and a handful of the People have ever seen a gun, but context defines it; the audience understands it is a tool of hurt. Their anxiety is almost tangible and Alice wonders how many of them want Lupe to recant.

"The sky is green," Darwin says. His words come slowly, with spaces between them. Each word is spoken loudly, with exactly as much emphasis as the word that comes before and that which follows. Ferociously, he tugs at Lupe's hair. "The sky is green."

"No," Lupe says.

Darwin strikes Lupe's shoulder with the butt of the gun and Lupe cries out in pain. The barrel of the pistol prods his temple. Lupe's voice rises and is clear. "The sky is blue!"

Darwin pulls the trigger of the gun. Its report is a sound effect, made offstage, but the deception is successful. When Darwin lets go of his hair and Lupe slumps forward, eyes closed, the People believe he is dead. Darwin stands before his victim, facing outward, his arms upraised. He remains motionless in the tableau of victory while the platform completes one slow rotation. "The sky is green," he says.

The People are silent. Ernestine dims the lights above the stage to signal that the play is over. When the lights come full again, Lupe is resurrected and smiles out at the audience. Darwin stands beside him, a hand draped brotherly on Lupe's shoulder. Together they bow.

The impact of the play is slow to dissipate. To break the spell, Alice applauds them, a small and hollow sound until others, almost reluctantly, join in. The clapping is not the spontaneous, asynchronous wave of approval that usually meets a good performance, but a sound as regular and rhythmic as the beating of a heart, a sound that, increasing in volume and tempo, seems to insist on life.

Ernestine joins Darwin and Lupe on the revolving stage. After a long time, the percussive clapping softens and breaks rhythm, finally stops. Playwright and players leave the platform then, but ending is not release. The People continue to stare at the empty stage until Alice goes to Lucas and asks him to dismiss them.

47

THEY'VE BEEN WATCHING A LONG TIME, awash in images and sound, before Michel says, "Here it comes. 'Nature Lover,' by Starfish." Seconds later, the announcer on the television echoes, " 'Nature Lover,' by Starfish."

There is an instant's still-frame—the band frozen in motion, fingers arrested on descent to keyboard, drumstick hovering above drum, mouth of singer gaped around a still-drawn breath, the red guitars aimed, neckward, toward the unseen audience, and in that instant, Bartholomew tries to read the photograph, to learn the Starfish of so many parts.

Then music comes, the organism moves, and the camera dissects the body into close-ups, fingers, lips, hips, eyes, while Bartholomew tries to perceive the whole. Fire overtakes them, their image lingers for a moment on a wall of hungry orange flame then slowly fades. The next cut shows what burns. A tree, trees, more trees than Bartholomew has ever seen together, and bigger, so big that climbing them, the flames appear to be consuming sky as well as trees.

The music Starfish plays is lyrical, even sweet, a ballad, though what its words say Bartholomew cannot take in because its sound claims him and the pictures fill his brain. The contrast between simple melody and shocking image sets up a tension in his nerves. The band becomes a concrete field sown with endless cars, a real field dense with flowers. For a few seconds, blossoms and grasses dance in the wind, then a shadow approaches, becomes a blade and severs flower head from stem. The band becomes two moist round eyes, the zoom out shows the animal, furry like Ringer, leg-less and possessed of flippers not entirely unlike Bar-tholomew's. Zoom out to whiteness, to many furred and flippered animals against a field of snow. People with clubs pursue the animals and strike them. Blood on snow fades to the red guitar. There is pain on the face of the singer, a female person, and his eyes are closed tightly as he sings.

Michel pushes the button on his control box and the screen goes dark. "Not bad, huh? The politics is pretty heavy, of course, but some things need to be said. And the fire's incredible."

"They must have had a very long lens," Ringer says, "to make the fire look so near."

"Twenty-to-one zoom," Michel says.

"What is the name of the animals?" Bartholomew asks.

"Seals. The baby seals in Newfoundland. You have to hand it to them. They found a way to get everything in."

Bartholomew and Ringer speak at once. Bartholo-mew says, "Why do the people kill the seals?"

"Did they use a tripod?" Ringer says.

Michel chooses to answer the technical question. He says, "They had to. All in all, it's a damn good tape, even though I didn't make it."

"The images are painful," Bartholomew says. "The tape hurt me. I don't understand why it's called 'Nature Lover.'"

"It's meant to be sarcastic," Michel says. "Ironic. Don't they have irony at your place?"

"What is it?" Bartholomew asks.

Michel thinks. "It's like the difference between how things are and how they say they are," he says at last.

"Showing that. We do it a lot in videos. Television is the perfect medium for irony."

"At the Place," Bartholomew says, "we use television to show how things that seem different are alike."

Michel smiles at him. "That's not irony, brother. That's something else."

"Does the band choose the images," Ringer wants to know, "or do they come from the makers of television?"

Michel shrugs. "Both," he says. "It can happen either way." His long brown finger taps a button on the control box and across the room the face of the television begins to glow. They watch another tape, another band.

Later, without the adhesive of television, Starfish shatters into seven parts—fourteen arms and legs symmetrically arranged on seven bodies, crowned with seven heads, driven by seven wills. They wander in a mist of fragrant smoke, tinker with their instruments, waiting for the rehearsal to begin. Across the room, Ringer sits on a battered black instrument case and talks deeply with the drummer.

The singer, a female person, approaches Bartholomew and stands, one hand on one hip, before his chair. His eyelids are green, his lips and cheeks red against white skin, hair stiff with frizz frames his pale rectangle face. Small silver fish-shapes dangle from his ears, flashing faceted green eyes.

"I saw your tape," the singer says.

Bartholomew nods.

"Far out," the singer says. "You guys ever trip?"

Silently, Bartholomew translates: a trip is a journey. They have not traveled far. "This is our first trip," he says.

The singer studies him thoughtfully, then reaches out

to touch Bartholomew's cheek. The brush of his fingers is studious and gentle. "I thought I'd be afraid of you." The red lips smile. "Actually, you're kind of cute. There's this movie I saw once, about a guy coming home from 'Nam . . ." The singer stops. "You don't go to the movies, do you? Jim says you've led a sheltered life. Me, too. Twelve years in a Catholic girls' school, surrounded by nuns." The singer laughs. "You ever see a nun? Old virgins in long black dresses. It makes me shiver just to think of them."

The singer shivers inside his silver shirt. His eyes are gray/blue under the greened lids.

"At the Place, we wear bright colors," Bartholomew says. "No one wears black."

"Nice," the singer says. "I used to wear black a lot. I did it because I was angry. Now, I don't know." He shrugs. "Now I figure you might as well live before you die. You know what I mean?"

"I never thought of black as dying," Bartholomew says. "For me, it's only the opposite of light."

"Light, life. I kind of like that," the singer muses. "Maybe I'll use that in my next song."

"Is 'After the End' your song?" Bartholomew asks.

The singer nods. "My dream. Seeing that tape was like *déjà vu*, you know? I feel like I made you up."

"Maybe you did." Bartholomew would rather be a dream of the singer than of the Fathers. "Sometimes I feel as if I'm someone else's dream. When things happen I know I could never have imagined happening."

"Yeah," the singer says. "Now that I've seen you, I'll never know if I imagined you first or not. I was tripping when I wrote that song. Now when I sing it, I'll always see you."

"When I hear it," Bartholomew tells him, "I'll think of you."

A door opens and closes; Jim Steward enters the rehearsal room and his presence is a magnet, collecting their attention. Conversations stop mid-sentence, or end in whispered ellipses. The Starfish finds its center. He is their Father, Bartholomew thinks in the silence before Jim Steward says, "Okay, you guys, settle down. It's time to practice."

"It was real nice talking to you." The singer's smile curves up, then flattens, signaling his disengagement. The band takes up its instruments.

48

CAPTIVE, keeper, captive, keeper, and so around. They occupy one arc of the dining hall's inner circle, and Alice stands before them, ordinary small Alice, drab in slacks and sweater. Alternating with the faces of the People, familiar and unique, the faces of the captives are too alike to read, though she can feel their attention trained on her and sense their fear. In no previous incarnation would she have made this offer, it is a risk she would not take. It is the People's offer, and she speaks for them.

"The Place," she tells them, "is a prison only if you choose to make it one. The People would rather welcome you as guests than hold you prisoner. If you agree to respect three simple conditions, you will be released from your bonds and free to move about the Place. The conditions are these. One, you will not attempt to leave the Place. Two, you will not attempt to communicate with one another. Three, you will remain always in the company of your keeper. Finally, we hope that you will learn and practice our code while you are among us."

She scans the arc and finds that only Kleig's face remains unrelieved, unsurprised. For a moment, his gaze is a laser, trained on her, before he shifts his eyes and begins a mute ocular consultation with the members of his team. One by one, they look to him, they question and receive his answer: *Refuse. I command you to refuse.* As Kleig releases each gaze, Alice engages it, willing her eyes to speak trust. The silence is broken when one of the captives, a physician, leans over to whisper something to his keeper, Boris. Alice watches. Kleig lobbies with his eyes.

"You may have some time to think it over," she tells them. "If you refuse now, you may change your minds later. While you consider, let us introduce ourselves. I'm Alice."

She nods to Peter at one end-point of the arc. "I am Peter," he says. Beside him the young woman, Laurie, looks perplexed. Peter touches her arm. Her voice is faint and breaks between syllables. "Laurie."

"I am Boris," Boris says. The doctor next to him says he is Roger.

"I am Adolph," Adolph says.

The captives are shy, naming themselves; they seem to feel both brave and silly. In a few of their voices, Alice imagines she hears a whisper of defiance. Kleig puts a period to the communal sentence. He will not speak. Alice is relieved by his intransigence, glad he is more stubborn than subtle. She expected it of him.

"We have no weapons," she tells them, "except those we took from you. We would never use them first. If you wish to be released, your word is bail enough." She sweeps the arc with her eyes, omitting Kleig, then swivels back to start again, a slower scan, person by person, heart by heart. She does this twice.

On the third pass, Laurie responds to her question with a small inclination of her head, a lift of eyebrows. Her face blazes red. Alice signals Peter, who wheels Laurie's chair to the center of the circle, beside Alice, and unties the cords which bind her hands and feet together, her body to the chair. Peter extends his hand to Laurie and helps her to stand.

Alice touches the girl's arm lightly. "Welcome," she says. "You may go."

Peter leads Laurie from the center of the circle, up a radius of aisle. When their weight touches the sensors, the wide doors of the dining hall slide back to let them exit and through their aperture reveal a brief tableau of winter sun on snow, of two backs leaving. At the center of the circle, Alice feels a sting of morning cold against her skin before the doors slide shut. She looks to the next captive. To the next.

In due time, three more of them choose freedom, and are released.

The gardens are white now, the lawns and stone pathways tarped by winter, the shapes of the shrubbery distorted by the weight of snow crystallized on branch and limb. A coat of snow subdues the evergreens, presses their arms close to their sides. The scene is frozen into a stillness that makes their whispers loud.

"When it's warm," Peter says, "I come here to work on my songs. The gardens are full of birds then, and I steal ideas from them." He whistles an example, one bar of birdsong.

Laurie's eyes explore a tangle of bare tree branches, ice-shiny against the winter sky. "I had a duckling once," Laurie says. "I wanted to raise it up, then let it go."

"What happened?" Peter asks.

"It died first," Laurie says.

"The problem," Boris explains to the physician Roger, "is to develop a mechanism that can position itself around the limbless ones." His drawings of the new derrick are splayed out on the table, and Roger studies them.

"There are two ways you could go," Roger says. "An infrared heat sensor that could read the body's position. Or, you could program a computer to drive the arm to certain given coordinates. Your subject would have to position himself quite exactly. The technology exists, but it's prohibitively expensive. You could hire an army of LPNs to lift your quadriplegics in and out of bed for the price of a prototype."

"It's my work," Boris says, "to help make each of the People as self-sufficient as possible. Isn't that the job of your inventors?"

"In theory, sure," Roger tells him. "It sounds just fine. But the numbers aren't there."

"What numbers?"

"The market's small. There aren't all that many people without arms and legs, and quite frankly, most of those there are, are indigent. Charity cases. Nobody's going to pay for research that isn't cost effective in the long run."

"Are you talking about money?" Boris asks.

"You got it."

Slowly, Boris nods. "Brother Alice told us that was the code of the people outside," he says.

Dorian stands at poolside to watch them swim, not because he fears they will try to escape or rebel, but because he's never seen such swimming before. Both outsiders swim the same way, belly down and face submerged, their arm strokes, alternately right and left, symmetrical and uniform. The music he plays in the poolhouse does not affect or inform their swimming; in two straight parallels, they race from side to side and back again. Their legs chop at the surface of the water, as if in combat, exciting two parallel wakes, and when their faces lift for air they look more desperate than satisfied.

Soon enough, they tire of their battle with the water, and Dorian passes them clean towels.

The small ones flock to him, in hungriness of touch, engulf them. The small ones are too young and too unquestioning to find Laurie exotic or forbidding, they tug and nuzzle without prejudice, and Peter sees on Laurie's face pleasure and fear together.

"This is a new friend," Peter tells them. "His name is Laurie." The small ones repeat the name, exploring it.

"Play music for us, Peter. Make us songs," they cry, and Peter sits, lips to the mouthpiece, his fingers poised above the strings. Laurie, too, sits down, and the small ones rush to colonize the lap that sitting makes. Like a living carpet, they spread around her feet, they lean against her legs.

"Sing with us," they command, as Peter plays the first notes of his two-voiced song.

Laurie shakes her head. "I don't know the words." The small ones laugh.

"There are no words," Peter says. To illustrate, he begins to play, and a chorus of nonsense sounds arises from the small ones, different in every mouth. The melody unites their babble. The one-armed child on Laurie's lap touches her cheek. "You sing," he says.

Laurie tries an embarrassed *la,* a reticent *loo.*

"Da da fa la figgily iggily ooo," the child chants in her ear. "You sing."

Laurie's voice rises. "Dee dum doo dum dee." The child bounces rhythm on her lap. Laurie wraps her trembling arm around him.

When the singing is done, the small ones turn to Peter. "We miss Barmew," they say, and, "Where is Barmew?" "When is Barmew coming back?" they ask.

Peter ignores the questions in Laurie's eyes. "I don't know," he tells the small ones.

Alice buzzes the television set in Adolph's room. Seconds later, the gymnast's face appears on her screen.

"Yes, Brother Alice?"

"I'd like to speak to Dr. Kleig."

Adolph wheels his captive within reach of the viewfinder and Alice sees Kleig's averted face. Already the shadow of new whiskers begins to obscure the contours of his shapely beard. The flesh around his eyes looks swollen.

"You needn't starve yourself," she tells him. "Food and water are available at any time. I'm sorry I don't have any scotch."

Kleig raises his eyes. The cable transmits the image of his scorn.

"Is that your answer?"

Kleig's face remains immobile.

"Have it your own way," Alice says. She switches off the set.

49

OUTSIDE THE PLACE, it is impossible for one in a chair to clean himself without help. Michel's apartment has no shower or shower chair, only a deep porcelain tub like the tubs where Louis scrubs vegetables or the People's clothes soak before washing. Bartholomew does not like to ask for help to perform so simple and intimate a task; outside, he does not like to ask for help at all because outside, the expectation that you in your turn will help others does not seem to be sufficient recompense for help received. Still, he feels unclean. Secretions of tension, of excitement and fear coat his skin, and the air of the city is different from the air at the Place, palpable and less benign. It leaves a scum on his skin, and he wants to be clean when he takes part in the concert.

The tub is filled with water, and the water is murky, less clear than the water at the Place. Bartholomew removes his clothes and waits naked in his chair for Ringer and Michel to help him into the water. He is cold, waiting, and cold retextures his skin into a grid of small cold-sensitive bumps. Michel and Ringer lift him gently. The touch of Ringer's metal hand on his bare skin is shockingly cold. The water welcomes him and his body relaxes in its warmth. Michel gives him a bar of soap and a rough square of cloth for scrubbing. They leave him to bathe. Call us when you're ready to get out. In the other room they play music and distance softens the music so that by the time it reaches Bartholomew it is lazy and evanescent as the steam that rises from the bathwater.

In his mind, he thinks of Brother Alice, and his body

remembers, too, it responds to the memory. What he feels is like the Excitement but more diffuse, a current riding his skin and easing muscles, warm in bone and fluid in his joints, a tingle of scalp and follicle, the taste of salt and ashes thirsty on his tongue. It makes his insides, his almost unimaginable organs ache, and Bartholomew cannot decide if this feeling is made more of pleasure or of pain; memory is torment, an unresolvable desire, yet he prefers it to the alternative of a forgetful body, mute and numb.

When the water around him is tepid and gray, Bartholomew calls out to them. The music changes, then they come. Michel spreads towels on Bartholomew's chair before they lift him into it, then gives him another to dry himself. Ringer returns to the music, but Michel stays in the room. Almost shyly, he asks, "Is there anything more I can do to help you?"

Bartholomew smiles. "I can dry and dress myself."

"Bartholomew, can I ask you something?" Michel's voice is tight and sounds smaller than usual.

"Ask me."

"I couldn't help but notice," Michel says. "You have a cock, but. Well, it looks like you've got something else, too. A slit. A pussy."

"I don't understand those words."

Michel looks away from him, at the window. "Sex organs. You know. It looks like you've got both. Boy organs and girl organs. Double equipment." He looks to Bartholomew to see if he understands. Bartholomew does not. Michel points. To be pointed at makes Bartholomew feel strange.

"These," he says. "Yes. I have two parts. For me, the Excitement has two parts."

Michel whistles softly. "Incredible. That's really

weird. What does it feel like? If you don't mind my asking."

"It feels good," Bartholomew says. "The Excitement is supposed to feel good."

Michel's laugh acknowledges and seems to try to exorcise embarrassment. "In my dreams sometimes, I have it both ways," he says. "It blows me away, but in my dreams, I like it. It doesn't seem weird then. When I wake up, I feel embarrassed."

"There is no shame in the Excitement," Bartholomew says. "It is a gift of Nature."

"Nature must like you." Michel's laugh is like the laughter of small ones. "But don't tell anyone I said so."

"I won't," Bartholomew says. He covers his lap with the towel. "I'm getting cold," he says. "I'm going to put my clothes on for the concert now."

Kleig lies on his bed, in his anger. "You look ridiculous," he says. "You are ridiculous."

Inside her silver suit, she smiles. It was not entirely to unsettle him that she wore it; the suit affords protection, too, from his interpretations. His clothes are twisted from struggle, stained with spat-out food, his hair is in upheaval and the smell of his sweat is sharp, a smell of hate and fear metabolized together. Her stern green gaze impales him, her voice is calm. "You find the People ridiculous, too, I suppose."

"You're not one of them." His voice insists on the distinction.

She states her own theme. "Your captivity doesn't have to be unpleasant. All that's required is cooperation."

"This is the twentieth century, woman. St. Joan is out. Understand that, or you'll burn."

"I want you to tell me when Harris Briggs expects to

hear from you. I'm especially interested in backup security. You didn't come here without a plan."

She sees, almost admires the force of will he exerts to curb his hostility. "It's not too late to ask for help. Just back off, and the Team will help you. You didn't think we'd just throw you away, did you? Not after sixteen years."

"It would be easier if you told me willingly."

"No one blames you," Kleig says. "Anyone would lose it after sixteen years in this asylum. If you ask me, they should have seen it sooner. They should have realized how stressful your position was."

Do not engage him, she warns herself, don't let him call the tune. She is beyond engagement and glad, glad that her expression is silvered beyond reading. "I hate to sound like the Nazi commandant in an old war movie, but there are ways to find out what we need to know."

"You can't stop me," Kleig says. "My work is too important."

"We found your gun," she tells him.

"After therapy, you'll see that our position is not only expedient, it's morally right."

She allows herself the release of laughter, a wordless cynicism escaping.

"If you give yourself up and accept our help, you can still lead a normal and productive life. If you won't, you'll die."

Her hidden smile persists, expands as she tells him, "I'm not afraid to die." She has not thought this before, but recognizes saying it that it is not only true but the true crux of the matter. The formulation brings her great serenity. Kleig, she realizes, is afraid to die. To die now would leave his lust for fame unconsummated. No cause beyond himself sustains him.

He knows it, too, and the knowledge unmasks him, reveals the symptomology of the infection of ambition. She sees a man enflamed by anger at the frustration of his desire, an angry man afraid to die. The tantrums of the small ones, confronted by the hard distinction between mine and thine, by the world's unwillingness to requite, even to acknowledge the enormity of their desires, are not so different. His body, like theirs, shakes to contain such anger. He says, "Maybe it would take death to satisfy your menopausal satyriasis," but his words are too blunt to pierce her silver scales or her serenity.

"You might as well know it, you're a lousy lay," he says. Her equanimity fuels his attack; he hallucinates toward an inadvertent truth. "I wouldn't be surprised if you were making it with half the freaks in this circus, you're sick enough for that."

The barb strikes and digs deep, stunning her, not with shame but with outrage at the desecration of something beautiful, a regressive alchemy that tries to turn health to sickness, gold into filth.

Her silence is too long, and he takes pleasure in it, smiles with the cold joy of a man who loves to win and loves to hurt, he smiles while she takes mental flight, sequestering Bartholomew and her best self beyond reach of his words or his imaginings. He stops smiling only when she produces the hypodermic, sticks it into his upper arm and squirts him full of Pentothal.

"You, Kleig, are the freak," Alice says.

The first band, what they call the warm-up band, stops playing, and applause for their performance warms up the darkness. The darkness is far-reaching; from his place in rear-stage shadows, he cannot see the end of it but perceives it uneasily as a living being with a mind, a will, a metabolism of its own. The darkness is filled with people, enough people to populate the Place many times over, and Bartholomew finds it impossible to think of them as individual people, with individual talents and opinions, with hurts and faults and wants, with love. Individually they are unknowable. The darkness welds them into a single other, unitary and mysterious to him. Beside him, Ringer joins their clapping, and Bartholomew wonders if this makes him, too, part of the darkness.

Externally, the dome is round, but the roundness doesn't persist inside, in the relationship of stage to audience. Here the stage is not set among the people, does not revolve, but describes one side of a rectangle, gigantic and immobile. Here there is no equality of sight lines, no parity in hearing, as at the Place, and the concert one hears from one seat in one row is not the same as the concert experienced by others elsewhere. People and performers are isolated by the space; one event takes place on stage, another in the darkness.

For a moment, the stage lights fall and the darkness is total, breathing anticipation, then under a fiery diffusion of red lights, Starfish takes possession of the stage, seven people claim or carry their instruments into the red light, moving friskily as small ones, as if they cannot wait to make music together, and Bartholomew likes their exuberance, more than he likes them, whom he has met, or their music, which he has come to know. Their appearance fills the darkness with shouts and whistles, with stamps and cheers as well as clapping, and the temperature of the body of the darkness rises once more.

Starfish dives into its music, as Leda used to dive into the pool, and frolics there, dips and darts and spins inside the music, and the sound they make mingles with the darkness and changes it into a denser medium, from air into a fluid where the senses swim. The darkness sways in time with them, it breathes in unison. When the first long song is done, even before the last notes sound, the darkness explodes into a laudatory rhythm of its own—stimulus/response—as if it feared a pause of silence between music making and acknowledgment of music made.

Song follows song. The musicians dance with their instruments, with their microphones and with each other, dance with the changing lights that play on them, dance with and for the darkness, they make music kinesthetically, the temperature rises, and the music they make is simple and for the most part optimistic in its sound, a music of major chords, largely free of the dissent of dissonance, even though Bartholomew knows, from listening to their records, that the words the music carries are sad, hard words, and he feels the paradox of their attempt, the anomalous synchrony they try to achieve between the raw and celebratory vitality of their music and the chantings of despair.

Knows too from listening that the two paired impulses—affirmation and negation—will not transcend their opposition, that the tension between them is unresolvable, by Starfish, anyway, or by *their* music and it frightens him a little to feel the tension this produces in the darkness, a collective tension so many times more powerful than his alone, a tension that cannot and will not be released by the mechanism which incites it, arousal with no promise of catharsis. The temperature rises, it grows hotter and hotter inside the dome.

At last it's time. Huge screens descend from the girded rafters to hang behind the band, along the sides of the rectangle, above the peopled darkness. Red, blue, green, yellow, purple—for a moment the kaleido-

scope of lights is dizzying, the band on its diverse instruments sends a blast of cacophony through the amps
that stills the darkness and into this silence the singer
speaks.

"Most of you know a song we did last year, called
'After the End.' You probably know too that there's
never been a video released of that song, for the simple
reason that no one could make one. Nobody could
come up with the right pictures to go with that song.
Well, now somebody has and we'd like to show it to you
tonight. For the first time ever. We want you to pay
attention, because we think it's dynamite." The singer
turns to the rest of the band. "Ready? Go for it."

And they shoot their music through the amps, an
aural assault, and Lucas appears on the hanging
screens, five screens, and is revealed and then becomes
nonLucas, turns into Clotho, turns into Peter, turns into
the nestling Hanford fast as the transfigurations of
manic dreaming change/change/change/change four
to the measure and Bartholomew feels his own heart
speed up painfully to serve the beat and in their private
darkness feels the touch of Ringer's flesh hand on his
arm and sees by the light cast off the screens the shining
of Michel's eyes, Michel beside him, and feels the throbbing of that other darkness accelerate   Small, sad-smiling Joseph Boris Ringer Brother Alice pulse by luminous (oh, Brother Alice) Lucas flashes bluely bluely and
in all its voices the band half screams half shouts its
message

> *Look Look Look Look*
> *Face it Face it Face it Face it*
> *See it See it See it See it*
> *You can't look away, baby*
> *No, not now*

don't look away
you gotta
face it face it face it
you gotta SEE
the light at the end of the cyclotron tunnel
don't look away, babe
I gotta say, babe
you gotta see babe
it's you and me babe
After the end.

"What is your name?"

He answers as a child would, obedient to the authority of the drug. "My name is Jerome Andrew Kleig."

"What is your occupation?"

"I am a geneticist. I am a behavioral ecologist."

"What is your intention here?"

"To learn."

"Be specific."

"To perform gross breeding experiments in tandem with detailed genetic analysis. To practice environmental resource patch management techniques on a human population."

"Is it your intention to withhold life-sustaining resources from the People?"

"On a selective basis, yes. It is the only way to learn."

"Do you prize learning above the lives of the People?"

"They are not people. They are an experimental population."

"Do you have no moral reservations about the effects of your work?"

"Morality is a behavioral management tool. It is a humanistic fallacy. It does not serve pure science."

"What provisions were made in case you met with resistance at the Palace?"

"If Harris Briggs fails to receive a positive report from me within three days, the Place will be taken by force. Tomorrow it will be taken."

"You will call Harris Briggs and tell him the takeover was easily accomplished. Things proceed according to plan."

"I met resistance. I have been taken prisoner. My report is negative."

"You will tell Harris Briggs that you and your staff were well-received, or you will die."

The drug coerces no more than truth. Kleig says no.

The saxophone sings wordlessly, and its voice is soothing. It mellows the darkness and the images on the five screens slow to its tempo. Bartholomew watches the images rise, pass, knowing always before the next appears what it will be, and it makes him sad that he can't watch the tape as others do, with fresh eyes and no expectations. It seems unfair to him that the creator can never experience his own work, that the act of creation excludes him forever from his own audience. Still, it's good to see the Place again, good to see the People there. On five screens, Ringer comes of age again, and the voice of Brother Alice speaks, amplified, over the song of the saxophone: *Your work, Ringer, is to make television. The People accept you, the People welcome you.*

Then the adagio is over. After respite, the band takes up its instruments and begins again the journey toward frenzy. The time is coming, the music races toward the time, carrying Bartholomew with it, hurrying him, when what he wants is to slow the approach, is never to arrive. Michel takes up the camera and readies it. Bartholomew feels Ringer tense beside him, feels fear, a hummingbird, invade his body. *Don't look away, babe. No, not now.* The beat of the music overrides his heartbeat.

Tomorrow. She can imagine no reprieve. The gears failed to mesh, time held them apart in their turning, *if* did not engage with *then* to drive the plan. She is left with her wanting and forced to recognize its ineffectiveness.

Bartholomew! Her mind searches for him, she imagines the city so she can seek him in it, she calls to him in all the places she can imagine him being, she demands his report, or that the universe report on him, but the only sound she hears is her own interrogation of time, the only information she receives is that her search is foolish and without hope. She will not find him.

Face it. Face it. Face it. You gotta SEE. They move forward, out of the shadows, the lights find and possess them, blinding them, and for the first time, Bartholomew understands that the darkness is not blind. He surrenders his sight to be seen. Two guitars flank them, the players swivel back and forth, toward them and away, heat rises from the darkness to engulf them, the music draws a semicircle around them whose completing arc is the darkness.

Michel crouches in front of them, his lens trained on their faces. The tape ends and their faces, his and Ringer's, appear on the screens, two pale faces changing colors under the changing lights, red blue green, four eyes dark against the backlight stare out to meet their own gaze staring back, five times multiplied, many times enlarged. As Bartholomew moves his eyes from screen to screen, his eyes move on the screens. He doesn't want to watch himself, or himself watching himself, and looks away from the screens into the audience, hoping to banish his image, but it persists in his brain, superimposed on the darkness.

you gotta see babe it's you and me babe

The band strums the time. The time has come.

It is time to tell the People. Alice on television tells the People what she must. Tomorrow. Our plan has failed. Tomorrow the Fathers come.

Applause attacks the song, overcomes the song and replaces it, a smooth transfer of energy from stage to darkness. In the transaction, the energy is exponentially increased. Sleek in tight white satin, the singer joins them at the intersection of cones of light. Bartholomew lifts his eyes to the screens and sees the singer's face on them, the singer's red mouth moving as his words come out.

"These are the people who made the video. They have a story to tell you, and I want you all to listen."

Bartholomew waits to be spokesman, while something rises wavelike out of the darkness and breaks toward the stage. There is a slight lag, barely perceptible, between the frontal approach of the roar and the microphones picking it up and feeding it back through the amps.

Listen! the singer shouts into the microphone, then whispers, *Listen.* The audience responds to the gentler exhortation. A sibilant silence falls.

Now, the singer tells him. Bartholomew fills his lungs with air.

"I am Bartholomew," he says. "And this is Ringer. I

am real. Ringer is real. The Place you have seen is a real place."

Between hearing himself speak and what he speaks emerging from the amps, the lag is significant and distracting. He echoes himself. As he speaks, a roar rises again out of the darkness and drowns his words. He tries to outwait it, but it feeds on itself, and is quieted only and provisionally when the singer intervenes.

Listen.

"The story I have come to tell you is true. It is not a pleasant story, but it is true. It may hurt you and make you angry to see how your leaders have deceived you. If you believe our story and wish to help us, then you must speak to your leaders, to influence them on our behalf."

The darkness does not listen. It prefers to speak, to roar. Bartholomew holds his story and waits to tell it. He has something to give to the darkness, he waits to give it, but it seems the darkness doesn't want it, or wants it less than it wants to reward *him*, with noise and energy.

The story I have come to tell you . . . Bartholomew begins again, but the darkness, the people in the darkness, reject his story. They accept him but reject his story. He looks to Ringer and finds him frozen in the light, staring out. If the people will not listen to his story, the Place cannot be saved. But the people outside have their own stories, and he feels himself becoming part of their stories. Their stories encompass his own, they become inseparable from his story.

Alice folds her hands in her lap and, sitting by the window to wait, wonders just how and just when the Fathers will choose to come.

The energy of the darkness seems inexhaustible, it comes to him and fills him. He tries to absorb the energy, to gather it up and use it to send his story back to them.

> *The place you saw is a real place.*
> *The People are real.*
> *I am real.*
> *I am Bartholomew.*

Half a beat later, the amps repeat it: *I am Bartholomew.*

It ends lovingly. She tries to convince herself of that.

50

RINGER SEES on five huge screens what takes place only a few feet away, the fast death as it overtakes Bartholomew. He sees the grimace, the gulping for breath, as if Bartholomew were suddenly thirsty and tried to drink air, he sees him slump forward, unconscious, in his chair. When he does, the darkness rises and advances, becomes thousands of regular faces and symmetrical bodies pressing in as it roars in one great common voice.

Ringer flees. Before the darkness reaches the stage, before it claims Bartholomew, Ringer retreats, he takes shelter behind a person-high amplifier, then breaks for the back of the stage. He parts the curtains and is gone.

Ringer knows the numbers of the highways that lead to the Place, he knows how to stand beside the highway and flag down a passing car; Brother Alice taught them that, as a mechanism for returning. He wants to return. The roar of the darkness is loud behind him and he does not look back.

Many cars pass him without stopping, but at last one does and he climbs into it. It is nearly dawn, a cold gray winter dawn when the car lets him off at the inconspicuous mouth of the narrow road that leads to the Place, and he walks for a long time on its rough surface, its ridges frozen crisp, its ruts filled with puddled ice, between the trees, before at last he catches sight of his home, still distant and surrounded by tall fences.

He hears them first, then sees them, a fleet of helicopters breaking into morning, arriving to hover like hungry crows above the Place, calling to one another in throaty whines. They strafe the ground with their lights. Ringer hears the report of an explosion. A voice cries out, and the helicopters sink lower and lower, until he can no longer see them inside the fences. He has come too late.

He is in time. No one has seen him, no one will ever know he tried to come back. He will return to the city. He will find Michel. The rotating blades of the helicopters still scream, the road is quiet and cold behind him as he turns and walks away.

51

HERE THE FATHERS REIGN as capricious gods. Their will is as arbitrary as it is absolute, and the People have no choice but to obey it. They are no longer a whole people, but people divided into groups whose members share common hardships. Some groups have little to eat, while others are permitted to eat only certain foods. Some are awake by day and some at night. In the dwelling houses, some groups live two, some three, some four to a room. In the dining hall, they eat in shifts, under a rule of silence, and with wide spaces between their chairs. Some groups are not permitted to go outside, while other groups are allowed to enter shelter only at specific hours. The members of some groups are always alone, of others, never so. Some groups have no work, and others have work that does not suit them. Only the Control Group lives as before, without constraint. They are the chosen of the Fathers.

There is sex at the Laboratory, though sex is not an act of love but a duty performed at the bidding of the Fathers. It is hard to feel pleasure under the Fathers' eyes, and it is forbidden in the act of sex, as elsewhere, to speak to one's partner. All pairings are selected by the Fathers, all matings ordained by them. Four nestlings have been born since the Fathers came to the Laboratory, and three of these have died.

There is no television to document or celebrate such barren lives, and the sets in each room, each workshop have become the Fathers' eyes, their ears, their ubiquitous voice. Five of the young have come of age without ceremony. There is no play. Before he died, Clotho's paintings grew dark and strange.

It is forbidden at the Laboratory to speak about the dead, or to grieve for them, but still the People contrive to keep their memories alive. The small ones are lulled to sleep by whispered ballads about a silver brother who guards their rest, and the stories are repeated endlessly in bits and snatches, whenever the Fathers are out of hearing: the story of Brother Alice, who met the helicopters when they landed and died for the People; the story of Bartholomew, the maker of television, and his apprentice Ringer, who left the Place to save it and were lost. Again and again, the older murmur stories to the younger of a better, gentler life before the Fathers came, and the People pray in secret to silver gods that such a time will come again.